The Perfect Pose at Hope Pass, Texas

by Terrence Kopet

PublishAmerica
Baltimore

First printing

ISBN: 1-4137-4172-X
PUBLISHED BY PUBLISHAMERICA, LLLP
www.publishamerica.com
Baltimore

Printed in the United States of America

Dedicated to Mary

Acknowledgment: To Hope Itself

I used to be able to take things as they come, and be grateful for them. Making the best of circumstances, trying hard, sure, like most do, but more or less not expecting perfection in anything. This being human life, after all. Then the envelope arrived, inviting me to go off somewhere. Years before, an old aunt had left a boarding house to family members who hadn't wanted it and hadn't wanted it, and then it became my turn.

The deed sat with a pile of other mailings for months, and it grew from a quiet murmuring haunt into a howling sheet of paper to my ear, and I read it again. The place was five hundred miles away, a small town in West Texas. Desert country.

After several more weeks passed, and feeling drawn to it, I decided to have a look-see. I made travel plans, said some goodbyes and drove out of the Sangre de Cristo Mountains where I live, then down through Santa Fe, Carlsbad, and across the state line into the wind desert. The trip was a long day's drive and ended — well, really, I don't think it has ended yet.

The road roughed itself into a long and flat laid that cut through indistinguishable miles on either side of it. Near dark

I came upon rusty railroad tracks near a sign that read "HOPE PASS 12 MI." While on this stretch, moonlight came and lit up a sandstone-covered earth and the blurry waves of heat the day's sun had left behind.

Through the vague light, I soon made out a group of structures up ahead. When closer, I saw many identical structures, all of the same conical shape and size, except for a long rectangular building that I immediately took to be my inheritance. As I drove past the last house at the north edge of the town, I entered a plaza that sat abandoned and wind blown. I knew then that my inheritance stood in a ghost town.

I parked at the front of the large house. With a flashlight in hand, I climbed the remaining porch board. Two large oak doors leaned at queer angles from their hinges and as I rubbed my hand across the grain of one of them, I realized that those who had lived here had imported goods, wood at least. Just inside the doors was a large room to the left and another to the right, this one with a long dining table standing in its center. I brushed away some of the sand that weighed down the table, but a layer of pounds and pounds of it remained, a gift the wind brought in through broken window panes.

My light showed a slender barrel of a hallway running down the center of the house. I followed it past chipped and peeled white doors on each side until I came to a hole in the wall at its end that was once a round window. Outside, the sands stretched all the way to where two identical-looking mountains stood, aiming up at the moon that was showing their heights to the eyes of a traveler.

I retrieved camping supplies from my trunk and set up bedding on the floor in the first room down the hallway. Sleep came by a hum unlike the Taos Hum I was used to. This one was soft and soothing and I was awakened only by the oak doors going bang and boom in the night.

I walked around the house in the early morning light and felt no personality in it to which I could introduce myself. I'd heard that previous voices of lives, loving tones and other, lived on in buildings, but I heard nothing. Only the paper deed I'd brought along had a voice and it still howled enough to keep my curiosity about this place barely alive.

When I re-entered the room where I'd spent the night, I saw that the dresser I'd noticed earlier and each of its five drawers was still tightly closed. The top drawer had a key sticking in its hole. I turned the key and opened the drawer, and the first light in years looked in on a few women's things—undergarments, ribbons, a photograph—and at the bottom of these I met up with a home-bound book, a journal, its covers made of hide and tied around with sinew that ended in a bow.

I picked up the book and stood flat for a minute, as my finger tickled the bow. I had a mind to let whoever owned it long ago to keep on owning it, but it wasn't to be, for I was with the howling deed in my pocket. I obeyed, pulled the bow and though I then had no way of knowing, what was opened for me that day was to alter my life by giving me a singular clear vision of something perfect in this world.

Inside the leather covers of the journal, in hand-printed script, I read:

e'll all be leaving here soon. People like me who have deep roots in our Hope Pass desert, others who came blowing in over the years, and our newcomer. Something happened here that brought ourselves home to us, but we won't be able to stay and be those selves here where the change took place. I have several days until our departure to put down on these pages what it used to be like here and how it has changed. Perhaps someone, someday, will read this and decide if what happened is worthy of note. It began a month ago.

Isabel Ritter

'Golden. Golden up and golden down,' is how Engineer Mert described the stretch of desert that led up to Hope Pass. He said it was the brightest place in the world to the eye. Sandstone grains lay in the sun for miles with more of it borne on the plains-heated winds as bright swirls in front of him.

The rails were the only entrails on this stretch of his route connecting his stops that the engineer mused were made back when our legendary founder, Mother Fate, had form and the earth was her playground. She'd left footprints for towns to rise out of and when the big strider stepped on where Hope Pass would one day rise up, she must have been blinded by the light near the end of a weary day, for this spot was sanded raw as steel and as hot as that metal when forgotten in the forge.

Number Nine barreled through as usual this time then puffed and groaned until coming to a half mile past the depot. Engineer Mert then backed her up and soon the engine and two cars stood flush with the platform where we'd all gathered hours before. We let out a cheer as Mert put his own feet down at Hope Pass.

'You missed the depot again Mert,' I said in a tease.

'I know, Isabel, I know. I'm trying.'

The miser waved his hand toward the baggage car. He swung open its door and handed down crates of oranges and plums, and mirrors and fans, part of his regular portage to our town. Strong men helped him unload this trip's water vats until only a large box remained in the car.

Then, leaning forward toward the tense choir of school girls, the engineer asked, 'What's my song this time?'

The half dozen singers all in a row each handed him a mud daisy and at the wave of Teacher Rachel's hand, they let out:

Hope springs eternal at the Pass,
And comes from round the bend.
We always see you when you pass,
But know you'll back up again.

'Oh yes, dearies, that I will. That I will.'

Someone asked him who was in the passenger car, a rare sight.

'A lady I picked up a couple of towns ago. Doesn't say much. Only that she'd let me know when she wanted off.'

Just like always, we all grew silent when Mert climbed back up into the baggage car and we remained so when he jumped back down with the large box.

Yea, the box. And each one just like it that the engineer brought every month as part of his delivery to the place he'd told us was more to him than way station. Here north of some places and people and south of other places and theirs. He'd tell us he loved us, hoped for us. He, in turn, was our big connection to any other place and the things he brought to eat, we couldn't grow but the hope he tugged along took deep root in our hearts. So, this day too, even though he'd passed the platform yet again, anticipation was high for the opening of the box.

Yeah, all those boxes. Everyone had a hope of what they'd contain. Years before, a boy here named Steve said he hoped that a long and sharp muskellunge fishing lure would be brought by the first Engineer Mert, the current one's father and initial hope bringer. And oh boy, Steve had said, he'd take that lure up to Cleavage Lake below the two mountains and though he'd known that there were no muskellunge in there, and that they grew large somewhere way up north, he imagined that the lure would somehow lure those fish to the lake and he'd have a heroic battle with one. It would drag him in ankle deep, but he'd fight right back and at last land that angry serpent with flashing jaws and teeth. Then he'd drag the big catch home and be a hero to the town. No such lure ever came in one of the boxes, and so no muskellunge followed.

When I was young I hoped for a smiling angel doll in the boxes and then one month there one was. More though, the doll darkened my mirror when I held it up beside my own reflection, to compare Hope Pass with hope itself.

Around here, when maturity comes, lures and dolls were left stranded outside our box hopes and the mature would hope that what was invisible and missing from here would take form and be contained in any of the engineer's cardboards. But this never happened and as one reached near middle age, hopes would revert to youthful visions and we'd again hold out for trinket or whimsy. And these hopers, me included, could see comparable expectations through the lines or wrinkles of other agers' faces as the day approached each month when the engineer and his cars would go roaring past the depot and rumble to a halt before backing up again.

Engineer Mert laid this latest box on the platform and as usual, made ceremony of opening it amid our quiet anticipation and the spray of shiny sands that the winds and his engine's roaring past the depot had caused to shake loose and fly.

He said: 'I know I went past again. And I know all of you know why. I know you wanted me to pull up shorter but I couldn't. Someday I will. I do my best. And this month – TA – DAA! Here before you, good and kind ladies and gentlemen of Hope Pass is ...'

And then, as slowly as a practiced-at-it man could do, he lifted from the box the only answer he'd brought for youthful, mature and once-again youthful surprise hope this month: his large hands held out a stack of lithotype pictures of a dell lush in green and peopled by picnickers who danced and frolicked across the scene, or sat on blankets cooing to a lover, and others sat at a hedgerow eating grapes, all under a bright moon sky that had only one cloud painted on it, a cloud pearly white and billowy, and a happy cloud, one could say.

The engineer placed a painting into a hand of each of the choir members who were momentarily transfixed by the joyous scene until they were nudged by Teacher Rachel to thank the gifter, and they curtseyed low.

I then read from the request list as I'd done for years, assigning goods to their appropriate homes or storage areas. When finished, I walked to the passenger car and greeted the lady traveler. I explained to her that the engineer would be staying for the night and another day and that there was room for her in my boarding house. She said that she'd been told this, and with a shy smile she thanked me and said she'd bring some of her things.

I walked back to where the box was and after grabbing onto it, I drug it up to the boarding house. Engineer Mert walked down the hallway to his room that I always kept the same. Its large windows allowed sunlight to blanket the room a second time when its reflective meeting with a wall-sized mirror spread the double glow over the same bed and nightstand. And over the 'Bless You, Mert' that spoke in turquoise stone inlaid in a wooden plaque that has hung over the bed since back when I made it when the first Engineer Mert began bringing monthlies to Hope Pass years before.

Mert later joined me in the kitchen where I fed him a square and where he'd take three more the next day, his routine stay in our town. 'Is she coming up or sleeping in her berth?' Mert asked me.

'She said she'd come up. Mert. The prints are charming.'

'Yea? Do they like them?'

'Oh, yes. How has your month been?'

'Just fine. Railing along. My route is my life. I enjoy the other towns well enough but yours is my favorite.'

'Well, you're our joy too.'

'I try Isabel, you know I try, don't y—'

'We all know.'

'One thing's for sure and that's that I'll keep on steaming down here.'

'Steam right past, you mean.'

I walked around the town with Mert the next day as he re-acquainted himself with Hope Passers and as he again took in the symmetry of what we'd built out of what he called a large footprint. In the place where a town square might have stood, we have our work booths, small arc-shaped structures that are placed to form a larger arc. Behind them are small stone houses that too, were build in the shape of arcs, as is the placing of them, so that everything in sight, except the rectangular boarding house, looks like the indent within a larger indent of a crescent moon. The indent arcs all face the depot, its time-tawneyed bricks holding up the east end of our entire purview. Our ancestors left no record of why they build it this way.

On the morning the train was to leave, the lady traveler allowed as how she'd like to stay for the month. After Mert carried the rest of her baggage into the boarding house, he helped men and boys load weavings, mud daily seeds, empty water vats, painted tiles and other of our cottage industry into the baggage car. He was handed the outgoing manifest of trade goods, our month's request list and deposits to be put in the Van Horn bank. Grateful handshakes saw him up into his car and soon the engine was stoked and running.

He pulled the whistle cord and then his handkerchief from a pocket. As was his habit upon departure from Hope Pass, he waved the cloth out the window and kept up this good-bye signal as he drove away from the depot toward a long curve of track that ran flat for a spell before rising north. And, as he'd let on to some of us, it was always necessary, after he left our town, to pull the handkerchief in to him where it landed on his eyes and stayed with their drainage for the moments it took for the light from his and his father's room, and for the faces of we Hope Passers to fade from his senses a bit.

Then he'd go to Van Horn and he'd continue his cycle of pick-up and delivery on a rail course that circumlocuted, as he put it—seeing it only from without and not high above— land the shape of that large being that had once spread herself out for the night, over her own footprints, on a gritty golden mattress.

We at the platform were silent in the time it took for Number Nine to amble out of sight and for its handkerchief to re-enter the train and dry eyes in the disappearing cab. It was, for us, the train of hope, an extra monthly cycle or consolation, I suppose, for what was missing at Hope Pass, for what the boxes never brought.

I closed the journal and sat down on my bedding. Looking around the room, I realized that this was her room and that her voice was still here. I also realized that I wasn't betraying privacy by reading her journal. She'd wanted it read.

Hotter than hell rolled in by midday and I lay on my blankets in a sweat. There were overturned, dirt-crusted fans in every corner of the room. I began to turn their knobs to "On," wishing for some magical electric force to turn the blades. Then I kicked a couple of the innocent and dumb things back to their resting places.

I took the journal out into the more ventilated front rooms and again began to read.

But was it a footprint after all? We'd all begun to question our Engineer Merts' view of this. For if the legend were so, wouldn't such a Mother Fate as she was imagined have chosen not only to step on and form but also remain where Hope Pass was to rise up out of the heat and sand? Remain to look after her minions? We see little evidence of her now and this for some good length of time that has passed, ever since the wells and women began to dry up.

We used to have plenty of offspring and water so deep and

sweet that we shipped it out to Van Horn and beyond each month. More water was requested from as far away as where that boy's muskellunge were thought to swim. But that all ended and then came barrenness above ground and trying to get beneath it too. And this Great Mother sleeps?

We'd started to look beyond to the outside and soon after each train of trade left, it was always the same, hope vision in our minds of rusty, clanky old pieces of wheeled iron that next time would come to an even stop at platform boards that may not have been sawn and nailed together into the shape of praying hands, but that's what they meant.

After Mert left that last time, I fed my boarders and the traveling lady, broke down the box and walked it to the last boarding room on the left, at the end of the long old corridor that Papa said his Papa had built and called 'The Journey of Life.' When I was young, Papa said that the hallway truly was a whole life's journey anyone could take if they could imagine it. The wooden floors, he'd said, were the miles to be traveled in life and the people boarded behind the doors were the mysteries of mankind. And, oh yes, the round window at the end of the hall opened to the brightness of the sandstone and the elevation of the two mountains that rose beyond and, 'Lizzy,' he'd said, 'it is the view of hopes and dreams and heaven far, far out there. See? Squint your little eyes Lizzy. There—do you see it now?'

I saw it for awhile until the night I overheard Papa telling Mama that he'd take good care of me if the dread caught up with her. I ran from my hiding place and stretched my arms around pale Mama who was shawled there in the heat of that July day.

The race ended only days later and after Mama was buried with the other Ritters, Papa took a snapshot of me with the red, tear-stained shawl wrapped around my shoulders. Afterward, I took the shawl to this last room on the left and placed it over the window in there. I decided then that as time went by, that shawl would preserve Momma's journey and new darkness in the very room where she had done her knitting, the shawl as well. Papa never said much about it, nor had he or I ever rented out that room.

Now stacks of flattened boxes nearly fill the room as they stand against either wall, forming another kind of corridor that leads to another kind of window. I placed the recent box on top of one of the stacks, turned and looked at the shawl over the window, then left the room.

Just like I do every month, after the box is broken down and stacked, I rival myself by taking the photograph out of my dresser drawer and looking into the eyes of the afraid and disappointed. I look upon those seven-year-old eyes, then up into my mirror at the same older ones and see what was remarked upon about them during my years away from Hope Pass.

Twice I went away for learning and twice I came back just like the others did. Years ago one of our young men died while away, but the others returned. Constable Betsy's Ellie left and I guess she'll stay gone. Some used to say it was the sweet water that brought us back and the reason a prospective spouse from elsewhere would follow one of us home and stay to be a husband or wife here.

That spouse migration dried up when the wells started to do the same. We'd tried to drill more but the reservoir was too low, so we began to sink at regular intervals, and drier and drier sticks rose to meet our eyes. Then we stopped sending out our sweet water and began having other water trained in, not much as first, but now it's vat after vat lined up in Mert's incoming baggage car.

We fill in our dry wells with the sand that we know won't be missed, rampant as it lay around here, as if it bred so well it would never dry up. It is bright as idea, though just like Papa had said, and we do use it for walkways and glass making and now it serves as cover for wells we can't do without.

Above our remaining fluid, shaped like an arc aiming its opening to the east, and not true south, as we too late realized that it should, is our town that sits in the middle of this desert. Yes, we're turned half way around from the flow of the earth and its waters. Mr. Ives thinks this is important but he won't explain just how.

The dresser drawer. I rose from my reading and returned to her dresser. During my earlier rifling I'd seen a photograph and it again lay under my eye. I looked at a red shawl and then at the little girl's eyes. She was past lost and gone, this little Lizzy. Only a mirror-less frame hung on the wall above the dresser but this must have been where my aunt stood in later years and compared her eyes. The shawl.

I set the framed photograph back inside the drawer and walked out to the hallway. The boards could still be seen, long but warped as they ran to the window hole. As I walked down the hall, I took a closer look at the doors and all were still standing or leaning on their hinges. The last door on the left was the only one that was closed tight. Real tight, for when I turned the knob and tried to push it open, it resisted. I put my shoulder against it and pushed the thing open, pushing a foot of sand away that had piled up. Inside, a steady stream of the late afternoon light ran down the middle of the room. As I walked into the light I realized that it was coming in from the window that the journal said was covered over. On each side of me was a pile of old cardboard with ragged edges and long, brittle flanges that had torn and were waving in a breeze that came in with the light that a shawl supposedly kept out.

As my eyes fully adjusted to the room, I saw that there was a caking of dried mud beneath a layer of sand on the floor.

Mud from where—just like in her room and pretty much everywhere in here? I neared the window and saw a piece of red fabric sticking out of the old mud. I bent down and tugged at it and soon I held the shawl in my hands. It was heavy and dark on one side and sun-bleached and nearly clean on the other. I shook it vigorously, loosening some of the mud, and then I took it with me and returned to the room where I'd left the journal.

Reading again.

Train gone but not forgotten, we settled into our month of chores and the gradual build-up of hope that will finally come down the tracks next time. We had the fresh vats of water, but they failed to dilute the concern of all that our own wells were shallower by the month, week and day.

Mud Daisy Steve stomped into the boarding house while I was preparing a meal.

'What are we going to do?'

I know he'd been worried about his flowers getting enough water, what with his own well level sinking fast on the very edge of the plain. I'd never before heard a panic or a high pitch in his voice. I asked him to have a seat and eat with us. I told him that we'd find enough water for his flowerbeds to get by until the train brought more in or until sky water fell, though this last only caused his eyes to roll.

At lunch, Mud Daisy Steve calmed a bit when it was suggested that we'd call a town meeting so all could report on their wells and we'd know exactly where we stood. My boarders, Mr. Ives and Teacher Rachel, agreed, and we gave the lady traveler a say-so.

We all knew—except the traveler—the entire town knew

that we must keep Mud Daisy Steve's flowers going at all cost, and a big meeting would give voice to this. It was for their grower's sake, yes—he was one of us—but it was more for what the flowers gave us that we cherished so.

After Mud Daisy Steve left the boarding house, Mr. Ives, Teacher Rachel, and I went around and told the town residents of the meeting and the time and place were set. We would meet that night at the boarding house and then we'd all walk to Mud Daisy Steve's flowerbed and take it in, in the moonlight. It was one of our newer traditions that the entire town would meet out there every full moon. Though a further view of the flowers during any moon phase was welcome.

I set down the journal and went outside. It was hot and windy. The gentle hum played. I thought that this trio of elements must never stop out here. I strolled the front of the arc houses that led south from the boarding house and noticed that, for the most part, their indentations aimed south, unlike Aunt Isabel's words had stated. Their color, each of them, had a darker shade from their bases to about halfway up as if they'd sat in something. I entered one, then another, and could see that caked mud lay on the floors, just like in the boarding house, and sand had blown in on top of it. There were furnishings left behind and some clothing hanging in closets. It didn't look as though the owners had left in a big hurry, yet they'd left many things behind.

At the south end of the town was a cemetery. The fence around it, mostly two or three posts and then a gap, then a couple more posts, kept nothing out that wanted in, so in I went. I stood among shiny markers, made so by the blowing sands. The graves looked to be shallow, for here and there a casket lid or corner showed itself through the sand blanket. I tried to read the names on the markers and made out a few. Some Bringases had lived here and some Greenfields, and I saw the name Ritter, my mother's maiden name. One had the dates 1888-1908 on it, but I didn't recognize the first name. I came upon two stones lying side by side and one read "Papa" Ritter 1875-1940—my aunt's father. The other one had only "Cecil Ri 1880-1931" still legible. There were other, older stones and more caskets that had somehow made their way to the surface. I felt a little more familiar with the town's provenance, standing near, perhaps on top of former town leaders, founders maybe. I noticed before leaving the grounds that no date I could read was later than 1960 and that was about the era of the furnishings and clothing abandoned in the arc houses and in the boarding house.

I returned to the boarding house, ate, and washed with water from a well out back. I didn't open the journal that night, but did walk around the house and began to like my new possession. I settled in the nest I'd made for myself on the floor of Aunt Isabel's room. Through the window holes came the gentle hum once again, as if carried in by the moonlight that was all of that—bright as any I'd ever seen. Almost sunlight, I remember thinking.

First light found me leaning on the sill of one of her bedroom windows. I looked past the well at the rear of the house and out onto the stretch of sand that glowed to the horizon. The hum was ever present and I tried to see it. The wind was only beginning to rise from its slumber, so I figured the hum was exclusive to it.

When I turned from the window and faced the house that was and wasn't in my possession, I saw it more as pieces than as some entity, whole and of itself. I knew that it held little for me. Perhaps I'd take the old oak doors and maybe the dresser back home with me. Perhaps not.

I sat down on my blankets and, being drawn to the story of the house more than to the house itself, I opened the journal again and was met with:

Some flowers do and some flowers don't,
Until finally one does, and the rest follow suit.

We met in front of the boarding house, men, women, and youth, and sat on the porch or in the yard. Mr. Ives said he'd sunk and that the eastern wells were nearly gone. He estimated that with the water that remained under the town and with the large vats-full that were brought in, we'd be all right at our normal usage for a few months anyway. And we could order many more vats by the next train.

There were voiced concerns about how no town could exist without its own water supply; counting on a train, on any outside source for something so valuable was risky. And, to tell the truth, that was the end of our meeting. We all grew silent at the thought of this dependence on the outside, yet for me at least, our monthly vigil on the platform, hoping for something in a box, washed into me as something way out of water's league.

We began to walk toward Mud Daisy Steve's house, this parade not so different from the usual way that brought the town together there each full moon for a few years now. His arc house is the north-most one and his flowers are north of that. Upon arriving there, we again were led past the arc house by Mud Daisy Steve.

Upon turning the corner, the glow of the flowers in the moonlight was as pearly as ever, white peace as it shined in contrast to its dark and sunken bed. The thousands of daisies blurred into one another in the circular layout of the garden and we saw one large flower growing out of a sand world.

As we drew nearer, individuals or groups set out on the tiled walkway that spaced groupings of the flowers. One could walk between beds that shot out in the shape of a daisy's rays as flower after flower arrowed outward and seemed to light up the night. Or you could walk the round tiled path that circled the central bed where many more flowers formed a mosaic of the daisies' disc. My skirt and shoes became lighted in the reflection of the glow and for a minute I closed my eyes and made believe I was one of the petals.

Coming back to myself, I felt that it was only a whimsy, me one of Mud Daisy Steve's petals. They, at least, were tended. The flowers had been an accident, I think, the result of their grower's outside years. For a jungle war, married out there. He'd been born here, left for learning, left and returned alone twenty years ago with a heart splintered and the points of the splinters showing in downcast eyes and posture. He'd been a gentle boy who'd hoped for big fish and who'd come back in need of some kind of glue to tack down the splinters. He built himself the last arc house way north and he bred himself a new flower under a sun that gave rays all days long and the moon gave its light in turn. Water had pooled and so his first glues, the phlox, flax, marigolds, hollyhocks and cosmos drowned.

Then came daisy seeds by train and he found a way to grow them in the muddy plot and it so happened that it wasn't long before their words grabbed hold of him. The first years' petals spoke 'She loves me, then she doesn't'. And he said he'd heard that before. So he took to ordering all varieties of daisy seeds and chemical pouches and mathematics books as part of his monthly trades. He'd cut and spliced and cross grew and the third year, twelve growing seasons here, one Miss Fickle said she did and meant it. More breeding and soon an entire bed of consistent love words came from his toil. He began sending out the true ones' seeds to El Paso and Las Cruces and by-and-by these flowers hence gained a following in eight states, in towns their breeder couldn't pronounce. He said he imagined that they grew well out there before being picked and coming to a stop in vases on the kitchen tables of lonely men and women, and that he could pronounce.

As the town's water level sank, his flowers' stems grew shorter and so the petals bloomed closer to the ground. But they still glow, this very night, his true-blue floating white glues.

'They're beautiful, Steve, just as beautiful as ever,' I reassured him.

'Thanks,' he said, 'they're all I got in this life.' He bent down, broke off a stem and handed me the flower. Then he walked across the tiles and did the same thing for every person there. As people started to leave the bed, he abruptly stopped upon seeing the lady traveler standing outside the garden, and who had, as we all could see, followed the parade from the boarding house.

Mud Daisy Steve bent down and broke off another of his daisies. He approached our visitor and handed her the flower. I heard her thank him and saw that he stood stone still, staring past the 'Thank You' from whence the words originated. As she began to turn around, I approached and touched her elbow. I looked at Mud Daisy Steve and told him that our Visitor's name was Rose. They self-introduced and Mud Daisy Steve asked her what she thought of the garden. She told him that she'd only seen such beauty in half-remembered dreams.

Rose and I began to walk back to the boarding house in a quiet fashion. I turned around before the garden was out of sight, and saw that the growing and breeding man was still standing in the same place, motionless like a statue.

I'd never heard of this flower. I closed up the writing and walked north to find this flower bed, if any remnants remained. The last house was as broken down as the others and had the same dark lower half on its outside. Its arc was turned mostly southward also and looked to be twisted at its foundation.

I walked past it and came to the beginning of the vast sandy flat. I kicked around in the low-lying area just beyond the house and turned up a tile. Then another, not far away. And more. I supposed that there were many of them, but the ones I found weren't in my circle or line, just lying under the sand willy-nilly.

Back at the boarding house, I walked through the kitchen, than began opening doors down the long hallway. Collapsed beds and more dried mud and sand held no interest for me, so I returned to the journal.

When large birds take to the air and talons curl up under their owners, the branches they leave bounce way up and down and spring side to side, never gently. The whole sky is alive and small birds perk. Even large rodents and beasts of the field take note that they're up there. Something's hunting, something's hunted, things have changed.

But some birds don't fly like the hunters, never have. Try as they might, they can't learn the trade from the crow or the raptor, and their course is a squiggly one, seeking shadows or leaves to hide under while the big eaters search the sky.

Indian Jon always comes down from the peaks during the month when the chokecherries ripen and the elk won't talk to him. He rides in on Bow and Arrow, first one then her offspring who carried on the name. They were Paints, loaded down with large and small hides and dragging long poles behind them.

He had a story too; we all tell tales hereabout, mainly because we stay close to our homes and our stories are our travels, at least that's the way I see it.

Indian Jon carries what we in the town carry, but he lives up in the two mountains, alone except for his horses, the hawks he talks about, and the ground animals he talks to. He was born of the Kiowa, he told me one night after we smoked his pipe. He was set on marrying the chief's daughter years ago but the chief refused him and so did the tribal elders. So he left and took his refused heart to Indian College in Santa Fe where he learned that he should leave there also and go live the old way, but not back in his home. He made of himself the Awoik tribe. He was their chief, their medicine man, and eldest elder. He said he led the war parties against bear and cougar, said where camp would be made, when to strike. He made the tribe's beadwork, invented and carried on its traditions and brought them down to town once a year to trade, and commune with that part of him that mirrored one of ours.

From a spot near his home in the cleavage between the peaks, he said he could look down and see the east-pointing arc town sitting on the shiny plain. And sometimes, on the hottest days, in the stream that rose from the sands, he could make out a large human-shaped figure that had spread herself out there.

He always brought his lodge poles and would put up a lodge behind the boarding house and hold sweat ceremonies for those who wanted his medicine. For days each summer we'd smoke his pipe, sweat and sing, and when we began to feel his medicine, he'd call a halt to the ceremony and retire to the small tepee he'd put up.

Sometimes he'd stay at night in a room in the boarding house, but I never asked him what occasioned this for fear of making him uncomfortable.

At the table this year I asked him if he'd tell Rose, our visitor, about the drumming up in his mountains. He told her that all was alive up there; some seen, some not, even the big drum.

'When I beat my drum I must bang it hard if it is to overcome the one that never stops up there. Never. I'm the only Indian up there. Animals don't drum, not even the coyote. It comes from high up, where I never go. I tried once— too scared.

'It's true. I headed up there one day to find out about the drumming. I didn't make it to the top. The higher I got, the louder it became. It got so loud that I couldn't pay attention to the rocks—where to place my feet. And the flying air gales are strong up there. But I kept climbing. My ears hurt. I went on anyway, until the mountain shook, and I almost fell. It was too strong. So I went back down.'

'What was it?' asked Rose.

'I see it only in lodge. I can't put words to it. It has no words.'

'And you think it's alive?'

'I don't say what I think. Used to be, I thought it was old holy men beating drums up there or old women beating sticks down in the center of the world. Might be, though, it's saying no one can go up there to find out until they are old and holy. I'm not so old and I'm not holy yet—just an Indian in the hills with large birds casting shadows down on me.'

I told Indian Jon about how our wells had kept getting lower over the past year and asked him about the water up where he lived.

'There is plenty. Snow water always melts down and into my springs. The moss and lichen are healthy. It's good.'

'We're just drying up down here,' said Mr. Ives.
Jon said that we could have his water if he could give it.

I had noticed the mountains. I lay down the journal and went outside to look closely at them. I could see that, at least from a distance, they were identical twins. Just like each other, with green most of the way up each one, and up past that line, they both showed smooth-looking tips, identical in size.

I moseyed around for a while, back to the cemetery, peeking in an arc house, and debated whether I should pack up the scarf and the journal and drive on home. I re-entered Aunt Isabel's room and began to put my things together, and when I picked up the journal, its cover fell open, so I sat and read some more.

f my permanent boarders, Teacher Rachel and Mr. Ives, I'm more concerned for Mr. Ives. He has enough already and now he so worries about the water. He's alone most of the time, even more than he realizes, I think.

He has told me that in his room at night, he sits at his desk and ponders his sores, their progress. He checks his head and neck first and then gets up the courage to roll up his sleeve to check on his problem's appetite. The large oozer grows very slowly and he showed me that it's now the size of a half dollar, and it looked like one too, I have to say — gray rises and reliefs that make a clearer face than does ceiling plaster.

We've all tried to relieve him. We've sent out for remedies and potions. Even Indian Jon's concoction didn't work, maybe because he's not the old, wise Indian yet, like he said.

One night about a year ago, as I was taking a late dessert to his room, I stopped at his voice, at the half-open door. I'd never eavesdropped on a boarder. Never. Papa said it was like stealing from the life's mysteries behind the hall of life's doors, that it was transom treason.

That it was not to be done. And I've not done it since that night when I stood in the hall of life, listening, instead of announcing myself or knocking.

'Still. Still and still, you're here. What penance you give me. Or she gives me. But she was the sinner when she said, "You're boring, Edgar." And after all I'd given her. The prestige of my position, the money, the house on Ferson Street that leaned to one side so at least when she was at home and stayed on the south side of the house, she didn't have to wear those lifts to stand level. But that grew old for her—oh yes sir—and she came to despise the whole other half of the house and me right along with it. The circles I brought her into. The operas I taught her. For nothing. Nothing but these damned sores.

'Now all I have are you, my pretties. My pretty, awful oozers. Face, neck, head, all up and down my body, what a mess. I'm a goddamned mess hall. Eating myself up. Hell fire in an Easter basket. I'm the restaurant, the table, the plate, the diner, the waiter, the chef, the menu. I'm the meal-ta-da. What to tip? What to tip? I see you, sores. Saw what you did when I tried to starve you out that first year—you stayed healthy and I only got skinnier. Saw what you did with my opposite tack of prime rib and French cake to get you in good moods— you ate heartily and I'm surprised you didn't give a burp of thanks, but you don't know moods, do you?

'My head. Well, lookie here at you again. And my hair— my saints up there, Peter, Paul, Matthew, Mark, Luke and dear caboose John. There were seven of you not all that long ago. Old Judas left, as expected. Only six now to stand out of the soggy sores up there, looking like lonesome reeds sticking out of their own private little swamps. You're almost all I think about, as if you have roots that grow in deep and conquer the inside as well.

'All of you oozers—pussing my years away. You've made a cannibal of me. I am a cannibal. Oh God, you have not intervened and kept me from becoming a cannibal. A cannibal. What's for dessert? What do cannibal men bring home to their families for dessert anyway? A carob bean to sit on top of a human appendage that he hopes won't roll off onto the ground before the eater is nearing full and can grab the bean and then pay fine compliments to the ingenuity of the fine hunter's cookless cooking?'

I set the plate down outside the door and swore silently. No, I promised poor Papa that I'd never again violate his transom code. I didn't know how to ease Mr. Ives' burden. And now the water worries for him. And he's taught us things in his five years here, and we haven't been able to help him. How much can a man take?

I got up and walked down this hall of life, looking in doors again. Inside one room there were bottles and jars made of glass or tin sca ttered and strewn and sticking up out of the sand. I pulled a couple out and though the labels were mostly gone, I recognized a cobalt blue jar from my mother's cabinet. I could read on one bottle's label: "Osha Root Cures All." A desk still sat in the room and still had frames of hand mirrors lying on its top. The mirrors were gone.

I noticed at dinner that Rose was spare with her water. So, later I took a full pitcher to her room and told her that she should drink as much as she wanted from her tap, that there was enough, for months anyway. We could all see that she was the quiet sort, or at least that she was quiet due to being new to us. She seemed mysterious to me, yet she lived behind Papa's mystery doors so that was all in keeping. I didn't know what to say to her beyond the water topic, and I looked long at her. She was small boned and the slate black hair that ran halfway down her back framed a waist like that of a teen girl.

Finally, I told her that we liked having her here and that I would accommodate any wishes she had. She asked about the town's history and my role in it. And after I went on for a while, she asked me if she could paint my portrait.

'Well, I guess so,' I answered. I told her that perhaps I wasn't much anymore but that I used to have pin-up legs. She giggled and said that she enjoyed watching me the past couple of days.

The following afternoon I sat in Mama's rocking chair that I'd brought from my room. I'd never posed for anything breathier than a camera and having someone pay attention to me made me tense. She sensed this and said she'd done many portraits of people and that I should trust her. Because she wanted a full-face pose, I had nothing else to do—could do nothing else—but look right back at her. As I watched her it occurred to me that painter and painted must learn a lot about each other.

She was so tiny compared to the size of the canvas and the easel that as I watched her, she became smaller and smaller in my eye. Very slender, delicate even. Her movements were short ones, whether moving or dipping the brush, or shifting her little weight on her stool. As her eyes moved back and forth between the portrait and me, I would smile at her out of some remaining discomfit and then apologize. She said I could smile away because she was most interested in a feature other than my mouth, smiling or not.

We don't get many people at Hope Pass anymore, only a stray or lost hunter from the city once every so often and usually they come for bullets, which we don't make or sell, so they move on quickly. As I watched Rose paint me, it glanced through my mind that she may be a different kind of hunter, the way she was quiet and watching and how she just came on the tracks and decided to stay a month in our isolated town.

After two hours she said it was enough for now, that she couldn't paint anymore that day. She walked to her bed and sat down on the edge of it, looking weary. I asked if there was anything I could do for her and she asked if I'd hand her a brush from the top of her dresser.

I walked to the dresser and said, 'Which one?' silently to myself, then aloud to Rose as I looked down and saw about a dozen hairbrushes sitting all in a row, lined up perfectly by size and brightness of color.

'Any large one will do.'

I started to hand her the brush and instead pulled back my hand. I asked her if I could brush her hair and she looked up into my eyes for seconds. Then she said yes. I sat down on the bed and she turned sideways.

Her hair was as straight as it was black. It was so soft, like corn silk. I told her I wished I could have hair like hers and not my curly old mop.

She giggled and said she liked my hair. I brushed from her forehead in long strokes all the way down to her waist where the growths ended. She was very calm and relaxed so I felt safe asking this mystery about herself.

Rose said she was born to a white mother and a Navajo father in Southern Arizona. I learned that she was an only child and that at eighteen years of age she'd gone away to art school and then to California to start her career. I told her that I'd been here most of my life and that hers sounded exciting to me. She said she'd lived only a half life all her life.

'What do you mean?' I asked her.

And this is how she responded: 'Once I left home, I seldom went back. I always seemed to be half somewhere, someone; half elsewhere, half someone else. Here too. Even in the things I do.'

'Hm...have you ever married? Children?'

'No children. I just turned thirty-six, so that'll never be, I believe. I was married once and halved my way through that.'

'My, my, you're awfully hard on yourself, aren't you?' I asked, while continuing to brush her.

'Oh, maybe. I wish I could be more like you—hopeful and dreamy. I don't go home anymore at all. When I left the city last week, I didn't stop off at my homeland. I just went past it, bearing east.'

'Where are you going?'

'I don't know.'

I didn't ask her any more questions and just sat there with her, brushing her pride while she began to hum and move her head and shoulders to the beat of it.

When I got up to leave, she cautioned me not to peek at the canvas, that I couldn't see myself until I was complete.

Half-life? Half-life? What a way to state it. What a way to look into a mirror. Or maybe the mirror gave her that thought, that identity. I again began investigating, and after looking into two rooms that looked to be uninhabited forever, I went into one off the hall of life that contained an easel, fallen to the ground. I looked at the dresser and no hairbrushes were to be found. Unless a critter had dragged any away, this Rose apparently hadn't left half of them behind.

We all kept up with our work. Hand industries went on under the canopied work booths. Teacher Rachel lectured the children. Mud Daisy Steve nurtured his flowers and the Indian sang out back, all under our beating sun and above wells that were sinking.

The wells were old, some a hundred years old, dug back when an old river that ran down from the mountains had dried up. Back when our ancestors had found valuable minerals in that riverbed and shipped them off in trade. It was known that wells dry and that they need to be re-dug, or new ones dug. Since Mr. Ives came and taught us about water tables, we'd become aware that re-digging didn't hold a hope for us. We always looked outward for our hope and as for water, why, all we had to do was confidently look up at the lush twin peaks and yearn for them to raise our water table back to where we needed it to be.

We didn't ... that's to say, I didn't, know why the drying up had to happen now. It was our time here and I felt that we deserved to live as our past generations had, without worrying about the vitals. Yet, funny ... we all knew all along that Hope Pass offspring had been dwindling for years and we were down to twelve girls and eight boys under the age of eighteen. And for years no new mates had been accompanying our outward schoolers when they returned.

All the mirrors we shipped in didn't help with an answer to these questions but we kept ordering more anyway.

I am able to see some things now—the shapes of our hollowed-out houses designed to welcome the east. The town had always depended on the train that pulled up to now pass, then back up to the depot of commerce, of commerce of the soul also, I believe.

When that train comes we adults just know that it must be aboard, the something that we've lost. We never talked about loss, all we had to do was count the children and look in the mirror. Nor did we talk much about the monthly train; all we had to do about that was count our remaining fruit and lately, peek into a water vat and we'd get primed and ready with hope.

No one uses the station-house anymore, haven't since I was a little girl. It's the only building here made of brick. Brick shipped in and built to stay. I wonder what would ever happen if someone actually wanted a ticket out of here. No one ever leaves for good. I suppose any exiter could use one of Mud Daisy Steve's flowers to board the train. They seem to be our pennant. Or maybe some of the sand. We wouldn't miss it.

I'd been a little curious about the station house. I walked over there. Up close I saw that it was built to last. The exterior with a little mortar, would be as good as new. When I stepped inside, it immediately felt like it still stood for something. She was right, though, it was—except for the feeling I had and deep, deep sand on the floor—hollow. There were wooden shelves still nailed to a wall and a few metal tins still sat on them. I saw a scrap of paper mashed up against a wall, a survivor of all the hollow and grit. It read: Row 5 Seat 4 / August 14, 1947.

It was at this time that the water pipes in the boarding house and in other houses, as we were to find out, sounded like they were coming to life. Some life, a life of thirst. Some racket to our ears and understandings. This new clanking occurred whether a tap was on or off and showed outwardly in the thinner streams of water that came from our faucets. Mr. Ives fretted quite a bit, stating that the pipes' next strategy undoubtedly was to just clank all apart and not another drop of water would come into this house.

We didn't yet know or even suspect that we'd all be leaving so soon, so the prospect of it wasn't mentioned. It probably felt to others as it did to me: how on earth could one single facet of life, albeit an elemental one, change drastically or eliminate our very lives here?

The noise was immediately burdensome and I realized that it drowned out the sandstone hum that we'd all rather taken for granted. We must have been living partly by its calming sound and now that the clanking put it to be in my ears, the memory of it grew louder.

I lay on my bed and hoped that a nap would overcome the new companion of air. As I looked up at the bed canopy, it waffled softly in the breeze that came in the window, absent its usually accompanying hum. As I stared at the white lace waves, they seemed to ricochet their movements back to me and so my eyes began to do the moving; over nothing so white and gentle, but over mountains.

To love God or granite? All the big-water stories and fish fossils on mountain tops. Peaks that are prayed to. Whence the water?

Then to water went my eyes. Water, water, water. More of ours disappears each day. We've lost so much. We pray for rain in this desert and designate God by the act. We can't divine ourselves, can't beg the twin peaks for it.

It floods in India, so tell Mr. Ives' newspapers. And the seas are always full. Compared to that, we only need drops. And drops and drops. What is a drop in a sea or falling from the sky? Is it a loner? Or a whole river? Poor troubled little drop, doesn't know where it's needed. It must have many names as it falls, soaks in, and gets called back up to join others in a cloud not of its choosing. And then on down it must go again, somewhere. In an isolated pool or in the China Sea or the Irrawaddy or in the Big Muddy I've read a lot about, or even in every Turtle Creek and Raccoon River than runs. The supreme changeling, the poor slave drop. Misnamed, though.

We don't want a sea or a river anymore, only our underground rivulet to draw from. Maybe we should have a bee and knit a big blue drop in the center of a large quilt and run it up a flagpole. Would storms see it and heed the call to duty and rescue us?

I sat up on my bed knowing I had my own duties to perform. I also must reassure Mr. Ives, Teacher Rachel, Rose, and Mud Daisy Steve, who has been taking meals with us lately. And myself.

After supper Rose joined Teacher Rachel and me on the porch for our evening sit.

Teacher Rachel said to Rose, 'This is all I do on weekends.'

'Sit here?'

'Yes, for years. They know where to find me on weekends, if there were any "theys," ' she giggled.

Rose wasn't volunteering anything, so I broke a short silence by telling Teacher Rachel that Mr. Ives dropped the stick today and said that best he could guess, that it was only a guess, we had enough water for six months in the well out back.

'I sure hope we can stay,' she said.

'Has the water here ever been a problem before?' asked Rose.

'Oh no, never,' answered Teacher Rose. 'It's gotten worse only the last couple of years. Slowly, and now …'

'Rachel, why are there so few children?'

'Shhh … we don't talk about that. It's family matters.'

'Oh.'

'Rachel,' I said, 'Maybe it's all our matters.'

'Well, you tell her then, Isabel.'

'It's been dwindling since I was young. Slow, slow

43

dwindling. Our children. Constable Betsy, Mr. O'Connell, Mr. and Mrs. Blass—they're all that's left of my school classmates. Rachel, the classroom was larger when you became the teacher than it is now.'

'Yes.'

'Do you have children of your own?' Rose asked Rachel.

'Me? Oh, lord no.'

'Not yet?'

'Yet? No, it's not for me. I'm past that age anyway,' responded Rachel.

'But you're young. Younger than I am.'

'How old are you Rose?' I asked.

'Thirty-six,' Rose responded.

'I am younger than you,' said Rachel. 'Only a year though. Do you have children?'

'No.'

'Did you ever want to, Rose?'

'Rachel, I thought I did when I was young. Nineteen or twenty.'

'I did too,' said Rachel.

I then told them that we were quite a pair and one—the three childless women sitting together on a porch because we had no sons or daughter to porch with.

'Did you marry, Rose?' asked Rachel.

'Yes, once.'

'Still marri—'

'No.'

'Did your husband want children?'

'Yes,'

'Not you?'

'No. Not by then. They'd have been half born, probably.'

I started to giggle, and then looked at Rose, hoping I hadn't offended her. She smiled and gave me a nod that it was all right.

She then said, 'Very funny,' and began to cackle herself.

'Not compared to me,' said Rachel.

'What do you mean?' asked Rose.

Rachel responded, 'This is what I do on weekends,' and at that we all broke out in laughter.

That porch. I'm going to miss that porch. And Teacher Rachel. She used to just start up talking and wander into a story about her family. They were from slaves and the only negroes, Buffalo Soldier descendants, who ever lived in Hope Pass. Her stories would run into things that she sometimes had to say didn't truly happen, but I believed them anyway. She told of how this or that ancestor felt unlike other Hope Passers and would want to be just like them until a Great Dark Being showed up. The being could be seen and heard only by members of Teacher Rachel's family and it would appear at regular intervals and loudly command those present to 'Look deeper, see deeper, be deeper.'

She said that's when her family began make-believe and I guess that's what made them our town's storytellers.

She is very dual. Fragile as a bird's egg in the eyes and in her slow step, but her neck is always straight and I don't think I've ever seen her bow her head ever an inch. Yes, I'm going to miss her and her stories and her neck.

I walked out onto the porch that nearly wasn't and sat down on its remaining board, dangling my feet in the hole left where steps used to be. I tried to feel those women sitting out here like they had, but there were no echoes or hint of remaining presence in the air, only the hum coming off the sands. I tried to picture a dark, childless woman telling stories true as can be, maybe. They probably were true to her, I thought, for there I was, making believe that her presence should have been right there on the porch with me.

I looked across the town arc, covered with sand. All for what had they built and kept this place up until ....until what, and where did they go?

My second day at Hope Pass was closing down so I kept after the journal. I though it would be best if I read all of it while still here, at the place Aunt Isabel had lived and left.

The occasion of Mud Daisy Steve dining with us had always been infrequent—he had things to do, he would say—and sometimes a year would go by. But that changed suddenly as he began to appear at the boarding house table morning, noon, and with flowers in hand for evening meals. Before anyone would sit for supper he'd walk into the kitchen, hand me a bouquet, less one he'd take out, and then walk his lone flower down to Rose's room.

At the table we all came to notice how Rose's lips would merely glide across the lip of her water glass and one evening Mud Daisy Steve made a point of taking noisy gulps from his glass.

'Yet,' he said, seemingly to no one in particular, 'there's water in the wells still and in our vats from afar. Drink, drink, and be merry, this day will never come again.'

It worked to a degree, for Rose's self-conscious drinking evaporated and she finished her glass.

During my pose in Rose's room the following morning, I noticed her mud daisies laying on the windowsill in bright sunlight. When I commented on them and told her that I had plenty of vases and ever jars for flowers, she said that she was drying them purposely, so she could take their seeds with her when she went. I told her that Mud Daisy Steve bags up his seeds and that he also sends out dry ones, that he had plenty, I imagined.

'Yes, I suppose he does, but after what he said to me at my door last evening, I want to keep these.'

I was silent for a moment and then Rose winked at me.

'All right, tell me.'

She giggled and said Mud Daisy Steve told her that her smile was the only thing he'd ever seen that looked like the potential that once showed itself to him in his beginning daisies.

'Uh oh.'

'Oh no. They were just kind words, the sort a lot of people use I'm sure. He said them in such a shy way.'

'Hmm…'

'Your portrait will be finished in another sitting. I think I've captured you—and maybe more, Isabel.'

'More?'

She said that she liked my eyes most of all, said to me that they were like a beacon's light but that the fog had rolled in and the brightness was held back. She went on to say that she saw that in Teacher Rachel's eyes, in Mr. Ives', in Mud Daisy Steve's eyes, in everyone's eyes whom she'd met here.

I left her room and upon entering my own, I went straight to a mirror. Fog? I asked myself. I couldn't see it in my reflection. I then lay on my bed and ran Teacher Rachel's, then Mr. Ives' eyes across my mind 's eye. Then Mud Daisy Steve's, and those of Mrs. Blass and others in the town. Fog? Fog? Is that what we're looking at in all the mirrors we ship in?

Accompanied by the clanking water pipes, I started to doze lightly as her words echoed in my ears. What else could one expect then, expect, expect, expect in Hope Pass, the way the train must back up all the time. The way our children have dwindled, or the way the wells dry up?

I set the journal aside at that. Lack of children, foggy eyes, drying wells. They sounded like zombies, a little. For the first time I tried to look at Aunt Isabel and the people she wrote of as she truly saw it; by removing myself in this way, by removing some big dumb eyes peering at the marks in the journal as best I could, I wanted these people to come more to life for me across the years.

They knew something at some level, and yet that something came to them foggy. Can fog, or hindrance to light, also reverse a light? Maybe they knew things in reverse, had gotten source mixed up with result. A savior train brought mirrors so they could stare at what their eyes bred; but what bred the eyes?

I walked out of her room and stood peering down the hallway of life. I went back to the room that had no hairbrushes and approached the window. Only blown-in sand resided on the sill as it did everywhere else. My eyes wandered to the floor beneath the window, and under a piece of nearly buried broken glass there was a tiny gray stick. When I bent down for a closer look, it announced itself to be a flower stem. It had short, dry shoots attached to it and a vague reminder of a clump of petals, colorless and flattened. I lifted the piece of glass and the once-flower lay imbedded in a dry caking of mud. I touched it softly and a piece flaked off, so I set the glass back down on top of the it, returning it to its preserved state.

He really did take her those flowers, then. I wondered just what did this Rose think was the cause of Isabel's eyes? Of the others'eyes? Did she come to see the cause of the fog, the children, the wells?

Back in Aunt Isabel's room, I brushed sand from the seat of an old rocking chair and sat in it. It still rocked to the grinding of grit beneath the bars. I tried to look out through my aunt's eyes but I could see nothing except an empty frame on the wall in front of me. And the rocking stopped.

She called me in to her room, coquettishly pulled the left side of her flowing skirt up over my face and walked me by the hand to her easel.

'Oh Rose! It is me!' And it was. My first look at the portrait showed straightaway that it was me who had been captured, as she'd told me. My eyes stared at my eyes-in-paint and I could see what she saw—the film, the Hope Pass film, I suppose. But past it, through it, there was light. Real light.

'Oh, I thank you so much!' I grabbed hold of the slight re-creator and hugged and held her for a minute long.

'It's been a pleasure for me, Isabel.'

Looking at it once more, something other than the eyes began to stand out.

'Rose, I'm not pretty like that.'

'No? It's how I see you. We see better than mirrors show.'

'But I'm forty-six years old and—'

'And a fine forty-six you are, to.'

'Ah.'

I hung the portrait low on the wall in my room so I could look at it while sitting in Mamma's rocking chair. All my free time that day was spent there rocking back and forth while looking at the me that dear Rose sees.

After dinner I took Teacher Rachel and Mr. Ives in to see it, then Indian Jon, and they all said how well Rose had done and how good I looked. Teacher Rachel said she'd like to have her portrait done also, Indian Jon demurred, and Mr. Ives said he'd refuse to be an agent of torture to paints or canvas.

When alone, I studied the picture further. 'Looks good,' they'd said. I saw that I wasn't what teenage boys would call an old bag, but I wasn't spring chickeny anymore either. I had some lines, my long fingers, and my curly hair that Papa used to say nest-making birds took a good hard look at.

Rose had told me during a pose that she gained so much when painting portraits because everyone has an animus, something fine in them, and she could feel what it was when she was watching their still faces as the new one was being created.

I became pretty vain for a while. I'd hurry from my duties and stare at the face in the painting and then at the one in my largest mirror. I moved the mirror so it hung right next to the portrait and I pulled the chair the closest distance from which I could look back and forth at the four eyes. I began to believe that I wasn't an old woman yet, that I was the same as when young, only a little more weathered, a little more foggy in the eye.

As I peered at myself, I forgot about the long fingers and the prospective bird's nest and tried to see what my animus was, what my fine thing was. I was a good cook and boarding house woman. I did my duties well and with pleasantness. I cared about and was loyal to Hope Pass and what it had meant to Papa. But what else could there be? I even loved my tenants and others too, in a way. I respected everyone. I stared again into the portrait's eyes. Where, what is my fine thing?

I didn't yet know that we'd be leaving Hope Pass abruptly but I knew that if or when we did, I'd be taking this portrait with me, for it had something to teach me about me. It became my search, my path to me, my mastodon of mystery.

I lay down that night, trying to sleep amid the bad choir pipe noise and began musing about my mystery. I dozed some and saw the great Mastodon of Mystery thundering along an environment strewn with what looked like large nets. Strong nets that the mighty creature bulled right through and it kept on moving into more of them. As it walked, some of the netting became attached to its legs and near its ankles, sticking like spider webs do to all that run into or graze them. After the creature passed nettings, the large part of them that didn't adhere to it fell to the ground. Traps, traps no more. But as it moved on, the clingings stayed attached to it and it dragged them along, hindered.

Once awakened by the pipes, I poured a glass of water from my thin-running tap and lay on the edge of the bed trying to understand this Mastodon of Mystery and the nets.

I did get some pipe-accompanied sleep and woke before dawn, still wondering about my dream. I robed myself and walked out of the boarding house and out back. I picked up a stick and scratched at the blanket that covered the tepee's entryway.

'You come in.'

I pulled back the blanket and saw Indian Jon sitting near his fire, looking straight out in front of him.

'Sit here.'

He motioned me to sit across from him and I did so.

'You are up early.'

'So are you, Indian Jon.'

'I rise very early each day.'

'Indian Jon, I had a dream.'

'What about?'

'A large animal. A mastodon.'

'Go on.'

'It was trudging through nets that tried to impede its movements. Strong nets, but it went right through them. It drug strands of it with him.'

'Was it paying attention to those nets?'

53

'No, yet they slowed it down. It just kept looking ahead as it moved.'

'A mastodon?'

'Yes.'

'Large mastodons used to walk this plain, I was taught. They were the largest animals here.'

'What do you make of me dreaming of one? What was trying to trap it?'

'It's said that the mastodon was the escort of Mother Earth, the only animal that was allowed to accompany her when she came up to the land. Only one thing can try to trap her animal and her too. Human beings.'

'We try to trap them? Why?'

'Indian Jon doesn't know all these answers. All I know is that human beings are the only thing that tries to trap them. Do you want to smoke the pipe with me?'

'No thank you. I … I must go get breakfast ready.'

I stood and walked over to the wall where the large empty frame hung. I ran my fingers along the inside part of the frame and there were small shards of mirrored glass. Next to this frame was a nail sticking from the wall.

I'd gained a little more joy at reading the journal and seeing the things she talked of, even a nail that the portrait had hung on helped inform my growing feeling for the life Aunt Isabel lived here. As far as the mastodon, I knew that they'd walked North America. But anthropological records and my own lack of belief in grand mysteries and Indian lore didn't allow me to give much credence to a Mother Earth who walked, or for that matter, one who made footsteps on sandy plains, or one who lay down and left a sleep pattern of herself way out here in an abandoned desert.

ots of us would quit our chores and join Indian Jon in his sweat lodge. His songs were part Awoik, part Christianity, and part a language no one nor even Indian Jon could name. I'd asked him about that language some years ago and he'd said the songs were just like him and I left it at that.

He'd sing prayers for all people everywhere and if someone in Hope Pass was ill or very old or grieving, the chanupa was filled many times and the drum and rattles were beaten and shaken more vigorously. The rocks were heated more and we sweat more for those in need.

In the lodge, I sweat away Momma's pain for herself. Sweat away, I felt her awareness that she was young and leaving what everyone deserved. I sweat away Papa's hurt too and prayed he wouldn't hurt anymore if he were aware that our town was drying up. Purified. For hours after, I would feel clean and feel that Mama and Papa were happy during that time. I never prayed in lodge for the train and its desired deliverance that belonged in the domain of hope, from us and not from God.

By the evening after a sweat, my old tethers remained loose, and for a whole month each year, I believed that Mama and Papa and I were together again.

Teacher Rachel would go to sweats but not Mr. Ives. He did try it once but his skin revolted at the practice. Rose went just today. She said she'd been to many sweats when young and with the Navajo and that she'd been in kiva.

At dinner, after her sweat, Rose thanked Indian Jon and gave him a beaded medicine bag, a bag she had kept with her all the years since she'd left the reservation. He told her he'd honor it and that he loved the greasy yellow beads sown into it and that those beads were hard to find up in his hills. We all laughed at that.

He invited us all for the next days sweat, said he'd do better. He told us that his Awoik medicine was still new in the world and it took time for new medicine to become powerful.

'But it's real,' he said, 'and the power is coming.'

I served Indian Jon's favorite dessert that night, cookies shaped like a tepee from a mold that I'd had one of the town's tile makers make. He liked the taste too, of ginger and chokecherry together. They all did, the empty platter said.

Mud Daisy Steve continued to loudly gulp his water and Rose continued to empty her glass.

I again explored the backyard, where she said the Indian had put up his tepee and lodge during those summers years ago. I was able to find a long pole under the sand and with it I prodded until I found a couple of charred rocks. The mud that half caked the rocks and its brethren mud in the houses and depot remained a mystery. I walked to the well back there and pulled the lever. First came sand from the nozzle, then water gushed out onto the ground and my books. I looked for the tepee cookie mold in the kitchen but it wasn't to be found.

I'd had some success succoring Mr. Ives and his growing water fears, so I turned my thoughts toward Mud Daisy Steve and his recent jollity. He'd returned from his war and built the arc house at the end of town and stayed there, alone. At first some of us feared that he might be dangerous. But he began coming around and the fear of him went away, as did our regard for him as being a recluse. And he responded to the train whistle and always showed up on the platform. He'd had the child hopes of big fish that bite and told me once that what he hoped for in the boxes since was forgetfulness, something amnesial, an emptiness.

Sometimes long periods would pass when he wouldn't be seen and then I'd visit him. Inside his arc house, only a lonely man could live. The walls were blank. There wasn't a photograph anywhere. On tables and stools were seeds laying on top of old newspapers Mr. Ives saved for him. I always felt safe with him.

This day, I found him sitting on his porch with a pile of flower petals at his feet and a bunch of the mud daisies on the step next to him.

'Isabel?' He kept his eyes peeled on the petals.

'Only me.'

'Um … I don't see you here too often.'

'I had some free time and just wanted to see how you were doing.'

'I'm doing okay.' Still the averted eyes.

'How are the daisies?'

'They're okay too. I believe they are adapting to the other water well enough. Ours is better, though.' He still didn't look up at me.

'Well, if you're okay, I'll be going. Oh, it'll be a fine meal tonight.'

'Here.' He handed me a mud daisy and turned to continue his plucking.

When I returned to the boarding house, I stood over my kitchen sink and plucked the flower and it ended in 'She loves me,' as usual.

I put down the journal and sat thinking about these people for quite some time. I guess Mud Daisy Steve could hardly be thought of as a recluse, given the remote nature of the entire place. Or could he? I wondered. I considered a couple of parallels, that a murderer could be considered a murderer by other murderers if he overdid it, or a dreamer colony might think an over-dreamer the real thing.

But the mud really had me stumped. I returned to the rear of the boarding house and pumped the well. Water. Fine-tasting water. I walked over to the next arc house and pumped that well. Dirt and sand came forth, then water. I moved from well to well at the rear of arc houses and except for one that gave only dirt and sand, each of them belched forth sand, then the water. When I reached the last arc house, I realized it was the last one, Mud Daisy Steve's. Water there, as well.

I walked around to the front, and after a thought of respect for privacy, I let myself in. I found it much as Aunt Isabel had described it. The same mud lay under a blanket of the same sand. There was a ragged old sofa and some chairs, stools, and two long tables, all sanded up. I walked to a back room, kicked away a broken piece of furniture, and came upon two large tin box containers with labels by a company in Chicago. Both locked.

I knew I hadn't inherited this house, nor the town, but I broke open one of the boxes nonetheless. Inside were ledger books and beneath them, photographs. I glanced through the photos but they were old and uninteresting to me so I put them back and closed the box. Returning to the main room, I saw that the walls were all bare. Not a single framed picture or photo or mirror.

I tried to let my mind go free and get a feel for this arc house, of Mud Daisy Steve, of the thoughts and hurts that must have gone on in here. There was nothing in it, though. Maybe too much wind and sand had blown in over the years, in one window hole and out another, I surmised. Yet, I wondered what does happen to thoughts and voices of the departed, dead or only moved away. To where do they go? Do they simply evaporate, adding up to nothing at all, or could they keep moving about, accumulating as this world of words grows older?

When I left the house, I went straight to the cemetery. I brushed sand and crud off a good number of stones long into the evening. There was no tombstone for Mud Daisy Steve, only other abandoned graves without a single flower in sight.

Mr. Ives, out of duty to a degree and more from dread I believe, continued to drop the long stick down into our remaining wells. It came back up with fewer wet notches and some wells were dry for the first time. We filled in these holes in the hope that any deep unclaimed moisture would move to the wells that still drew. As this continued, it didn't seem quite real to me, or overly tragic, and I reasoned that this was because I, and the rest also, always had that short, month-long hope wait for our train that would remove our woes.

So our wells continued to dry under a Father Sun that never took daytime naps or hid behind rain clouds. Hot rays beat down on work canopies and continued to shine up the sandstone.

No one was visibly getting ready to leave Hope Pass, but if they were like me, there was thought of it. The anchoring thought for me was that at least we had months to decide such things. I intended to cook my best, and try to do my best so that nature might notice and then help us here. I spent much of my leisure hours staring back and forth between my portrait and the mirror. Then one day I took out the photograph of me in the shawl and my eyes would move among three things then. I vowed then that the portrait would go with me if I had to leave someday.

Where would I ever go? Van Horn? That way I'd be close and could return if the wells filled back up. Could go to Austin where I schooled. I wondered how out of place I'd be. But what about the rest? Where would Mr. Ives go? He has no one anywhere. Neither does Teacher Rachel or Mud Daisy Steve. Or this Rose, I think. Maybe no one here has anyone elsewhere. I can't just let Mr. Ives and Teacher Rachel leave here with so much aloneness out there for them. Maybe we can all go together. The three of us.

Yesterday Mr. O'Connell said we should all go up to the mountains with our belongings, but Indian Jon wasn't asked about that. Besides, a lot of us are set in our ways here, so much so that it would be difficult to live roughly until we could build and smooth things out up there.

I hope we never go unless absolutely necessary. Not after all the trains training us with anticipation . How would we ever get along without the train? Maybe we'd all end up living right near railroad tracks somewhere. Bet we'd look funny, running down to a station at any and every old engine whistle. Ah—we'll get the whistle here. Our train will always show up. That's what it's going to do.

Sleep was becoming harder to come by, chased down hard as it was by the noisy pipes. A soft tap on my door last night was welcome and when I opened the door, Rose was standing in the hall of life. She said she'd always been a light sleeper but nothing like now. We agreed that no one could yet tell if we'd get used to the bad symphony.

Sleep or no, she had something to say. She told me that last night, instead of standing with her door ajar while accepting the nightly mud daisy from its grower, she'd let him in. They sat for a spell and she said that Mud Daisy Steve still didn't look at her eyes while they talked, that he stared a little lower. She was pleased with the company, saying that anyone who could invent such beautiful flowers who spoke so well, who spoke so consistently well, must have harmless intentions, very honorable ones, even.

I asked her last night about her marriage and after she bent her head downward a little, she said that it was more of her half-way by-way of life. She began to tear up, so I took her by the shoulder and pulled her to me. As I held her she reached into the pocket of her housecoat and pulled out a hairbrush. I took it and began to brush her beauty vines. I told her that I had no intention of combing only half her hair, just as the creator hadn't had any half-way intentions when he was forming her beauty. She continued to weep for quite a spell, then she stilled.

I couldn't exactly place this Rose to me. In a very short time she had felt like a sister, a friend, a daughter, the wise woman, and even a spirit to me because of her smallness and large gentleness.

After she'd gone I looked though my mind's eye at her small bones, all nearly covered by her ranging long hair. And I could tell that there was an enormous heart in her. A strange feeling came over me then. I felt like I needed to look at things, Hope Passers, me too, differently, to look to inner size in proportion to outer. If Rose's size could belie, maybe everything did.

While I was preparing breakfast the next morning, Mud Daisy Steve walked in and poured himself some coffee.

'Isabel, I hope Rose doesn't leave on the next train.'

I told him that that was also my hope.

'You know, Isabel, that I stay to myself a lot and I don't ask things of people.'

'I know,' I responded.

'But I do want something from her.'

'What?'

'I see something in her, or feel it—something I've felt before.'

'Like what? For a woman?'

'No ...not exactly. No, it's something else. Something more than that.'

'Most people look into others' eyes for a feeling about them, Steve.'

'She told you?'

'Yes, She's not put off by it. Just mentioned it, that's all.'

'Isabel, it's her mouth that I look at.'

'Her mouth?'

'Yes, have you ever noticed how she smiles? Only part way. And at this table, have you noticed how she eats?'

'Well … no, I guess not.'

'She barely puts a spoon or fork in her mouth. She holds back just like …'

'Like what?'

'Like everything is small and level. She talks small and level.'

'Is that bad? You sound critical.'

'Well, no it's not bad … it's too bad.'

'In what way?'

'It's … it's like when I started to breed my daisies. They had more to them than they were showing, more than was being asked of them, sort of.'

'Steve, I don't know what to say. She's a fine person, I feel.'

'Oh, me too.'

'I will say that I was thinking about her last night, er, early this morning. She does have something large in her tiny person.'

'Maybe that's it!'

'Think so?'

'Maybe there's something that keeps her …um … keeps others …all of us—closed more than we should be.'

'Well, if you find that kind key or gentle wrench that can open people up, let me know.'

The other diners came, and I watched Rose as small and level and different than that inside.

became even more respectful of my boarders after my mistake at Mr. Ives' door, so because of my concern for him I took to knocking on his door with pretty flimsy excuses. This time I told him it was his dessert night and the look he gave me was some sort of cross between a smile and a dumbfound.

I sat on his bed while he sat at his desk. I told him that we were going to hold out as long as possible. He said that if waste away he must, he'd thought all along that it would end at Hope Pass.

'I've never seen past this place. I've never even considered any other town or area. And to tell you the truth, Isabel, I don't know how I'd ever find someone like you.'

'Ah, Mr. I —'

'Ah, nothing. You've been good to me. You leave me my privacy and need I tell you that your cooking is splendid.'

'Well, we'll just hope we can continue on as always.'

'I admire your spirit, Isabel. I know you've lived here for … about ever, but I measure those wells. They're going down, down, down. And fast. It's true a town can't live on trained — in water.'

'Well, until—'

'Until the pipes explode because they can't stand their own

sound. We've all noticed how they have drowned out the sandstone's song. I was struck by that song as soon as I came here. It has helped me some. Soothed my skinny some.'

I asked him if he was the same.

'No, it won't stay the same. It's a slow eater but it makes progress all along. It's a good thing I'm tall or I'd be a lot more eaten away by now.'

'Nothing helps?'

'No. Teacher Rachel comes by and rubs an old salve potion on me, but even that doesn't help.'

'That's too bad.'

'Well, it helps a little. Her touch … being touched is what does help. Imagine, that fine woman not being afraid her beautiful skin will be infected by mine. I thought that she'd be my last hero but I'm afraid that won't happen now.'

I told him that if we ever did have to go, we could all go together. All of us.

'You know, I would have expected little else from you. Funny isn't it, how all of us here go through the actions of life—the lack of passion here that we've spoken of before— and yet, there is care and kindness in most everyone in Hope Pass. Hard to figure—for me anyway. People have been good to me, that I know.'

'And you've been good for us, too.'

'Me? I have? How?'

'Yes, you.'

'How, then?'

'You've taught us a lot—the origin of the sandstone song, and the reason for it. You taught us about the water table. Topology—now nearly everyone in town knows all about it. And what about the story of Scipio—we can all recite that history. Then there's—'

'Okay, okay. Trivial things.'

'No, not trivial things. Besides, have you thought how much dignity you've shown us?'

'When? When I'm not in a snit and cussing like hell?'

'Well, no, not then. But in the honest way you bear your burden.'

'Nah ....'

'Yea.'

'I consider myself to be an old curmudgeon who is, well, preoccupied most of the time.'

'Maybe, but you've still helped us.'

'Well, thanks Isabel, for saying so.'

'I hope you bring your best appetite to supper tonight.'

'Why?'

'I've made your favorite dessert.'

'Really?'

'Yes sir, French chocolate cake.'

'I guess I'll just bring that big appetite then. Appetites I mean, ha ha ha.'

I laughed right along with him for a few seconds, than left his room. I recalled that once, on the rare occasion when Mr. Ives ventured out of doors in the daylight, I overheard children snickering at Mr. Ives' sores. He'd overheard them and bellowed for the little orphan urchins to mind their manners. After being so reprimanded, one of the children asked of another, 'What's eating him?' And I thought to myself at the time, 'Plenty, but he keeps up.'

In the room that had been Mr. Ives', I sat at the desk he'd sat at. The mirror was gone, so I looked into the wall, trying to imagine being eaten alive by myself. Isabel said that he was getting sadder, and who wouldn't. It couldn't have been leprosy, as well as he ate, and it wasn't spreading grossly or else that would have been mentioned. If salves and potions and all sorts of remedies didn't work, it must have been blood caused. Maybe in this day and age he could have been helped.

I was finding that I was beginning to care about these people, but how much? More than motion picture characters, more than characters in novels even. And yet, they weren't exactly or quite real to me. They came to me at a new remove. They'd be very old or dead by now. And if dead or alive, dead or alive elsewhere.

I again walked back to the cemetery to make damned, er, undamned sure none of these people alive during the writing of the journal were in there. None were. They all left and no one came back to the place that was home hope syndrome, the supposed last place, for them. Never came back?

After the cake, Mr. Ives retold the story of sandstone for Rose's benefit. He explained the cause of its ethereal song and of its age-old reputation for providing clarity to those whose ears live near it and of its purported ability to temper and make calm what was inside those ears.

Rose commented that she'd noticed that everyone in the town seemed quite calm most of the time and that everyone went about their business in a slow, no-rush fashion.

'Are we rife with clarity?' Teacher Rachel asked her.

'Well now, maybe I don't have enough clarity myself to make that judgment,' she answered with a wink.

A wink that brought smiles or laughter to us, and then everyone grew silent. I don't know what thoughts that silence brought into the others' heads, but I remember that mine ran to clarity, then to the fog in our eyes, what it is, and how could people, near the sandstone song or not, be very clear out here in the heat of the desert and especially now with our water problem.

Mud Daisy Steve broke the silence by saying, 'Well, I don't know about clarity, Rose, but did you see anything calm hereabout when that train came in?'

More laughter.

'Our water's clear,' chortled Mr. Ives in one of very few times I'd ever seen him speak with humor in his voice. Then he began to speak and as we always did when he spoke, we listened.

'Yes, the sandstone probably influences us; it's no occult knowledge, really—this, like I said, is a very old legend—and the older the legend, the more people who have given it credence. Now, however, I don't believe it is having its usual effect because—well, I should say I don't feel it's having its usual effect upon me.'

'What do you mean?' asked Indian Jon.

'Simple, as you all know, I don't, can't venture out very often in the daylight—and yes, I too used to wonder why I didn't go live in a cloudy, rainy climate. But as it is, I stay in my room and that song is now drowned out by the damned noisy, damned water pipes playing their damned awful, damned music.'

'Yea, they are something all right,' said Mud Daisy Steve.

'Omenic too, I'm afraid,' said Mr. Ives.

'I don't want to talk about water tonight, okay?' said Teacher Rachel.

After all had gotten up, I cleared the table and took the remaining cake to Mr. Ives' room. He answered the door with his sleeve rolled up. He began to thank me for the thoughtfulness when I reminded him that he'd already thanked me a couple times. 'Well then, I thank you on behalf of my oozing little partners.'

His head and eyes headed south, so I said goodnight and left him.

When I went to my room for the night, I stood by a window hoping the good song would come in. After pulling Mama's rocking chair close to the window, I sat for a long time with my hands on my chin and my elbows on the window's sill, looking and listening out. I watched the moon rise on its own arc routine and light up the sand until it was clear and bright a long way out there. But no song.

Mr. Ives must be right, I thought, the sand must have had an effect upon us. People here have always been slow moving, temperate. Yes, temperate, save an occasional show of passion and of course when the trains whistle blows. And I guess we've gotten slower and slower over time. I wondered if other towns, once they age, slow down like people do when they get older. My, my, I then thought, people get so slow that they don't even move anymore, like Mama and Papa out in our cemetery. Do towns die?

Maybe we've slowed so much here without even noticing. All the unmarrieds here, all the children not here. We do have compassion, even Constable Betsy, but passion itself? Kindness, here? Yes. Care? Yes. Don't we? We must—look at us when the whistle portents our boxes. The air is thick with care then. Yes, we care.

When I finally rose from the window in the middle of that night, I took out the photo Papa had taken and looked at it closely. I cared so much for dear Mama. Since I've grown, I've cared about all the feelings she'd missed out on by slowing down completely at such a young age and with a husband who cared for her and a little girl who needed her care. We all care. Mr. Ives cares. Teacher Rachel cares a great deal for her students and she even nurses Mr. Ives some. Mud Daisy Steve cares for flower and mud and beauty amounts. Neighbors Louise and Ben care. Everyone cares. Even Engineer Mert.

I put on a housecoat and carried the photograph and a flashlight to the cemetery where the very slow ones stay. Out here the song was steady. I shined the light on the two stones where my slow ones are. I told them that I have been living, moving, even if slowly, for them. Here in our town. I swore to them that that would never change, even if I were to leave Hope Pass. I knelt down and kissed the stones and felt two kisses come back to me. The moon was finishing its tour when I rose to go home. All along the curve of arc houses pipe noise could be heard, drowning out the song all over town.

It was in Rose's room the next day when Mud Daisy Steve knocked on her door. She let him in, smiled, and walked that day's flower to the windowsill where it joined the others. He stood shy and said he didn't want to be out of place. Rose and I both told him to stay and he only waved a hand and said he'd see us at supper.

I began brushing Rose's hair again, this long mane of hers having become the conduit between us, and as it seemed from the first time, this activity bred offspring of warm feelings between us.

'Does he look you in the eye yet?' I asked her.

'He did last night, after I asked him to.'

'Oh good.'

'Yes, it's better. I asked him why he hadn't been able to do that before.'

'What did he say?'

'Isabel, he said that he had a hard time not looking at my mouth, that it reminded him of his early daisies.'

'A good thing, no?'

'Well, I guess so, as much as he cares for his flowers.'

'What do you two talk about, Rose?'

'Oh, our pasts, like most people do. His flowers. Our

futures a little, though it doesn't seem that anyone here knows much about theirs.'

'You like him then?'

'Yes, quite a lot. I sure must find how much that is, pretty soon too.'

'Why?'

'Isabel, Mud Daisy Steve said something very strange to me last night.'

'How strange?'

'He said that the job of his life was his daisings, and that he'd like to try the same experiment on me.'

'Maybe we should talk about something else.'

'Well, maybe.'

'Do you want to talk about it, Rose?'

'Mmm...mmm.'

'It's all right, you can just sit here and I'll brush.'

'You're so generous, Isabel. I love it when you brush me.'

'I love it too. Makes me feel giving and close to you.'

'Isabel, are you lonely out here in the desert?'

'Lonely? Maybe I don't even know anymore. There's no unloneliness to compare it to. Except my boarders. And except when the Indian comes down here each year. I like Mud Daisy Steve and I like almost everyone here. '

'Do you—'

'I was very lonely once I'd completed my schooling and returned for good. I had a boyfriend out there. Brought him back here. Papa liked him. Asked him if he'd like to stay and help run the boarding house. But he left. I never knew if it was because it's desolate out her or whether our running to the train made him uncomfortable.'

'That's too bad. Did you ever see him again?'

'Never. Yea, it is too bad. Or was. I don't feel all that lonely, though. Besides, I don't have the great legs I used to. Would you believe that people would comment on them?'

Rose abruptly turned to me and looked at what she could see of my legs.

'Pull your gown up a little.'

'Rose!'

'Go ahead.'

I lifted my gown above the knee and Rose said they were still great legs, 'Not skinny like mine.'

I patted her on top of the head and liked her even more.

'You know, Isabel, it wasn't so difficult for me to ask that question.'

'What question?'

'The gown lifting. That's sort of what Mud Daisy Steve asked me to do.'

'He did!'

'Yes, that was last night too.'

'That's awfully soon isn't it?'

'No, not that. That's not primarily what he's after.'

'Then what?'

'He told me—oh, you see, I'd told him all about my being a half-way person. "Old Half-Way Rose," that's me. So, anyway, after he told me that he wanted to experiment on me and if I agreed, he wanted to know exactly what he was experimenting on.'

'Hmm—I'm a little lost, Rose.'

'Well, he said that nature makes daisies fine enough. But that he found a way to open them up and not exactly out-do themselves but to reach wider meaning and wider beauty. And he said that he saw by my half-way and my only half-open mouth when I talk or smile—he even noticed when I eat—that there was even more meaning and beauty down lower in me than shows.'

'That's what he said?'

'That's what he said.'

'Did you—'

'No.' Rose giggled and shook her head from side to side.

'He wants to study your mouth and your other?'

'I believe he does.'

'All in the name of experimenting?'

'I think so.'

'Are you going to?'

'Isabel, I don't know. It's odd. But, he is so gentle and sincere. And he said … you won't tell anyone, will you?'

'No, what now?'

'He said they're the same, almost exactly the same.'

'Rose, I don't know if I can handle this.'

'Like I said, I think it's so very odd too.'

'I'll say.'

'Don't think bad of me because I laughed. I don't know if I will do it—if I even could.'

'Well, I'd certainly have a difficult time being studied like that.'

'However it goes, I'm the old Half-Way Girl. I doubt if his experiment would even take with me.'

I began to laugh. Then uncontrollably. The whole idea, the very idea of it, the very act of discussing it bubbled out of me. A brand new thing and it shook me.

When I was able to compose myself, I was the one who apologized for laughing. Rose only smiled and said that we've both been treated to something way out of the ordinary.

'Yes,' I said, 'Strange science indeed.'

Through laughter-teary eyes I said my goodnight. Later in my room, the laughter returned a couple of times. The pipes clanking and the experience kept me up most of that night.

I do wonder now if I'm eavesdropping. I'd never heard of such talk, or ideas. She wanted someone to read this for some reason. I guess I'll stay the course and find out what the reason was.

I looked up at the ceiling that she often stared at into the night. A smile came over me and I began to laugh. Strange place, this Hope Pass. Trains with boxes, flowers that always say love, weird science. Now deserted, these people, their box hopes, skin diseases, tepee cookies, houses shaped like arcs, wells that were wet, then dry, now wet again. Where did they go?

At this time, the first water grumbles were heard. Not the general concern about the sinking wells or the future of our town, but about waste. Mr. Ives continued to take his flashlight out at night and sink and in the mornings the news was spread. No one mentioned Mud Daisy Steve's flowerbeds, but another person received words.

Indian Jon used water to rock-heat his lodge and he and all his lodge guests used too much some other townspeople now said, in the replenishing of their lost sweat. We did need to drink a lot of water after a ceremony, gulping for half the day afterward and that's what set them off. Several people went march-like, to the rear of the boarding house to confront Indian Jon with their concerns. Afterward he came inside the boarding house and announced that he'd be leaving.

He said that he came every year for the same reasons: to pray, share his Awoik medicine, trade with the people, and be a Hope Passer for a short while. He told me that the marchers were rational and calm when they presented their protest to him. He said he'd take his tepee and lodge and go back to the mountains early.

At this, I went out and approached Constable Betsy, the leader of the protesters, and asked her if she thought that she'd done the right thing.

'Yes, I do,' she responded. 'We've all cut back on baths, on our birdfeeders, our laundry. If we don't waste, we can hold on longer. Maybe rain will come. Indian Jon said he's got plenty of water up in his mountains.'

'You don't go to lodge, Betsy,' I reminded her.

'No, and that's got nothing to do with this.'

'I happen to know that that Indian prays to his Great Mother for rain, storms, and high wells for us every single day in that lodge.'

'It hasn't rained a drop, Isabel. I haven't seen a storm cloud venture anywhere near here.'

'I know, but to chase him away like that—'

'Oh, Isabel, we're not chasing him away. It's the lodge.'

'Well, he's set to leave before his usual month stay is up.'

Constable Betsy turned and resumed the work she'd long pursued under her canopied arc booth. She shipped in small bottles labeled 'The Truth Inside.' After she'd drink the truth, she'd soak off the label and glue a mystery clue to the outside of the bottle. Then she'd write the answer on a small folded piece of paper, place it in the bottle and cork it. To twist and turn and unfold the paper and cipher the answer through the glass was the challenge. A challenge people out there apparently enjoyed for she's stated that they are in novelty shops in many places.

At dinner we discussed water, the protest, and the tepee cookies that again were coda to our meal. I told Indian Jon that I couldn't stop people from saying or feeling what they wanted to. Although for my part I would sleep on dirty bedding and wash clothing even less often and that way he could keep his lodge open for the two remaining weeks of his stay.

'No, I should go,' Indian Jon said.

'Now I've been here nearly all my life and I've never so much as told anyone what to do. My, my, I don't even tell my boarders to strip their beds on a given day or to show up at table time or they miss out, no sir. If they want to do things their way, the way they like it, then I like it too. And my Mama and Papa were the same way. But if you leave here now, what with these wells, who knows if we'll even be here next year. No one's ever left in an unwelcome way before. I've a mind to go out back and pull Bow and Arrow up into this house by his rein and sand guard over him with my quilt beaters. And then you'd have to stay and then no one will have ever left here by being unwelcome.'

'Here, here!' shouted Mud Daisy Steve.

'I'll help her stand guard,' said Teacher Rachel.

I looked around the table and saw that Mr. Ives and Rose were nodding in agreement. Indian Jon looked around the table and something came into his eye.

'Why Indian Jon,' I said, 'Is that a teardrop I see in the eye of the Great Awoik Warrior and medicine man?'

'If so,' he said, 'It's the first moisture I've been able to bring here. I'll take my lodge down tomorrow. I'll stay for the train.'

The tear scene was joined by a couple more single drops, and as we realized his moisture production increased even more, we cheered him.

I told the table that it was natural for the people to be worried and raise a little wool; we were worried too. But it was just as natural that we keep ourselves, ourselves to all degrees possible. And I reminded them about Constable Betsy's known generosity towards Ellie.

The next day Rose asked me about Constable Betsy and an Ellie. So I told her that Ellie came to us when she was sixteen years old. Orphaned, to live with her last known relative, Old Doc, her great uncle. But Old Doc died soon after and Constable Betsy took the girl in. Ellie was a pretty girl but when she came here her teeth were so bad, so headed every which direction in her mouth and gray and rotting. Worse, her dream was to become a kissing booth girl with a traveling carnival. Constable Betsy told her that with those teeth and their odor, Ellie would have to pay the boys to kiss her. 'That's okAY,' the girl had said. 'No it's not,'Constable Betsy had replied. Soon Constable Betsy quit ordering in the flower print dresses she loved to wear and instead she paid to have a dentist from Van Horn come to Hope Pass for a day each month for a year. Ellie ended up with straight, non-stinky pearly whites.

When Ellie turned eighteen, sure enough, she went away to pursue her dream. I told Rose it has been over ten years since and her letters to Constable Betsy still state that the young men pay to kiss her. She travels all over the South with the carnival and with each letter she sends, accompanying it is a bright flower print dress for Constable Betsy. So bright are those dresses that we joke that the only thing brighter is the sandstone shining up our desert.

Beneath the toiling sun and waves of steam that rose from the cooking sands, our wells continued to dry. The pipes in the boarding house groaned more steadily and soon they never ceased. The noise now completely drowned out the sandstone music that had always come in the windows as accompaniment to our days and sleep and dreams.

Not being able to sleep, I rose from bed one morning and on the way to the kitchen I ran into Mud Daisy Steve emerging from Rose's room. He greeted me warmly and then walked out of the boarding house door. All that day Rose stayed in her room, saying through the door when I'd ask if she was hungry, 'No, thank you. I'm not. I have some thinking to do and I have snacks in here.'

That evening she came out to the porch and sat quietly as Teacher Rachel and I discussed the changes taking place and our lack of sleep. Teacher Rachel said she'd packed a bag and this news reverberated loudly in my ears. So, It 's really happening, I thought. Things could actually come to an end. For all of us.

Rose opened up and said she'd be leaving on the next train that was due in less than two weeks. She said that she'd become very grateful for all the kindness she'd received and for the townsfolk allowing her to see us and get to know us—for taking her in for a time. She said she'd be heading north by train. She had a map and decided to get on the old Pecos line that ran east into central Texas.

When Teacher Rachel asked how far east she'd go, Rose said she'd keep going until she met people like those that lived in our town. I scooted across the porch until I was sitting next to her. Then I placed her head on my shoulder. I patted her on the head and told her that she brought something nice to us and that if we couldn't talk her into staying here, then we'd miss her when she went.

'I'll miss you, too. I've grown fond of you, and you too, Rachel and Mr. Ives. Mud Daisy Steve is a dear. We talk about so many things and he has ideas I've never heard before. And you know what? He has taken an avid interest in my childhood, part of his trying to figure out my half-way life I suppose.'

I asked Rose if she would tell us about the early years.

'The reservation was hard. But my mother and father were good to me. I told Mud Daisy Steve about all the dolls they'd given me.'

'Tell us.'

'My mother used to buy them for me from white stores in the town and my father would bring them home from trips. The little Indian dolls were my favorites when I was very young. As I grew older, I wanted white baby dolls because I could see Indian girl faces, real ones, right there on the reservation. They could see after a time that I liked the white ones best so I was given more of those. They all had round faces with pink or blue little moving eyes that looked back at me. The eyes looked so happy. I used to stare and stare at them. Such pretty eyes. I would then imagine that they wanted to leave the dolls and go out to where they looked, to what they were looking at that made them happy.

'I kept all of them until I went away. I walked all about the reservation, giving one of the dolls to each little girl I knew of.'

'That's a beautiful story, Rose,' said Teacher Rachel.

'I've often thought of them. The little girls, too. I've wondered if many of those girls left as did I.'

'You don't know?' asked Teacher Rachel.

'No, I don't. I know it makes me look bad. My father and mother were killed in a car crash not long after I'd gone away. I used to wonder if they had gone somewhere out of their way to get a new doll for me and that's where the accident happened. Soon after, well, I suppose that's when I became a half-way person, as I call it.'

'But why?' I asked.

Rose teared up a little and said that she hadn't return for the funeral. That she'd never gone back.

'Do you ever think about visiting?' asked Teacher Rachel.

'I have. I almost went there on this journey. Just to walk around and see where my mother and father are buried and to knock on those little girl's doors and see if they were still there. But I thought, what if at all those doors I would be met by grown Indian faces with eyes sad because they were still there? So I rode all the way through Arizona to El Paso and then to here.'

She left off talking when Mud Daisy Steve walked up to the porch.

'I had a nap today, outside under a canopied booth. Aren't all of you getting tireder?'

'I think so,' responded Teacher Rachel.

Rose then got to her feet and she and Steve went into the boarding house.

After they'd gone, Teacher Rachel said that more talk was probably going on in town than ever before due to the pipes' depriving us of sleep. And I agreed it must.

When I finished reading about Rose's dolls and the porch meeting, I again went out and sat on its remaining half-board, dangling my feet in the hole beneath it. As it was the other time, I couldn't feel the presence of the women out here. I got up and walked around the town. It was hotter than hot and the desert song blew warm in on the breeze. I caught myself supposing that the breezes and winds must have a purpose. Everything is said to. Maybe they rhapsodize as avatar or as warning or only as natural phenomenon. Heard but not seen, blowing away , and who really could state a wind's intent?

didn't notice exactly when it stopped. It was the same as when you realize that a great pain or grievous thought is gone and has been gone for seconds, a minute, even a long time. There must be a name for that gap in recognition. There should be. I think I'll call it 'thank you.' Yes, thank you. The pipes were quiet and I sat up in the dawning in my fitful-sleep bed and looked around. It was true. And the sandstone song again played in through the window. I went to my bathroom faucet, turned it on and saw a wide steady stream of water coming out. It had been a year since it flowed like that. I rushed out to the kitchen and it was the same from that faucet. 'It's back,' I gushed, and upon stepping back into the hallway of life, I encountered Mud Daisy Steve. I told him about the water and asked him if he'd noticed that the pipes were quiet.

'There is? They are?' he asked slowly.

He walked slowly toward the door, feet close together with a more languid posture than usual. Before he left, he turned and said, not to me or anyone else, 'I'll let the flowers gulp now to the end of their petals; they've been stressed.'

My left foot wanted to turn and run down the hallway of life and rejoice out loud but my right was more curious about Mud Daisy Steve's reaction. I went to the door and went out onto the porch.

'Well, you don't sound very excited, Mr. Flower Lover.'

He didn't even turn around and continued to walk away in this un-lope he'd taken on.

Back in the boarding house, all was quiet except the song. I thought that because of our recent lack of sleep, that my roomers must have been catching up right then, so I put off the rejoicing until later. I walked down to the window at the end of the hall of life and through the rising light of day I saw the great expanse of plain move or sort of quiver a little. I blinked and rubbed my eyes and looked again. Again I saw a gentle sway, slow-moving billions of sands moving easily up and down. One after another. Then it was still.

I thought that maybe an earthquake had happened deep in the ground. Back up the hallway of life I walked and I once again found myself out on the porch. No one was about yet. The world out there was as it had always been, serene—oh, maybe a little past serene and touching gently upon lonely. The song and I held down the fort for a short time, held the lonely at bay until the first worker showed up at her booth.

'Constable Betsy, is your house quiet?' I shouted.

'As a mouse, Isabel,' she shouted back with a smile.

I brewed the morning coffee and went to my room to write this down, but it would have to wait, for Rose appeared at my door. Well, really she turned the knob and walked right in.

'Rose?'

She said nothing and stood inside the door holding an empty glass of water, swaying side to side. She was nearly as pale as pale and then her knees began to wobble. I rushed to her and caught her up in my arms.

I coaxed her over to my bed and struggled to get her up there.

'Rose? Rose, can you hear me? Rose? What's your name?'

'Water.'

'No, it's not! It's Rose!'

'Mmm … yes. Water. Please … water.'

I hurriedly got a glass of water, held her back in one arm and she gulped it down.

'Water.'

She drank a second glassful then asked for more and drank it. I didn't know if I should go fetch Constable Betsy, our something-doctor, leaving Rose alone, or keep filling her up.

'You're going to blow up if you drink any more.'

'I … I lost a lot.'

She was starting to gather and her gulping slowed to long sip after long sip. Her eyes were the like of which I had never seen before or heard of. They had their usual dark brown color but they were so bright in their darkness and moving in lazy waves.

I propped up pillows and bent over her just inches away. I watched those eyes glow and move until I began to think she was in real trouble.

'Rose?' Are you warm? Rose! How do you feel?'

She wouldn't answer and I couldn't leave her, so I screamed, 'Someone, anyone, Help!' But Teacher Rachel and Mr. Ives must have been sleeping.

'Rose, are you having a stroke?'

'Tee-he,' she giggled once.

'Rose, where were you born?'

'I…I was born in … a place called Hope Pass, Texas!'

'Rose, quit pulling my leg.'

'Oh, it is true. I was b… born one night in a little town somewhere in … in the desert. There were other people there. They loved a train. Sure did. They loved a train and hoped for something on it. It was in …'she tailed off to sleep.

Constable Betsy read her temperature at 98 degrees, said her vital signs were okay except her pulse was systolic. She said that could be caused by a lack of sleep and beyond that she would only be guessing.

Rose gradually returned over the course of the day. I fed her in bed and barely believed the volume of water such a tiny woman could hold. From the time she came into my room near a faint until later afternoon, she drank over 200 ounces of the stuff and let very little liquid go. Later, I tucked her in to sleep and walked outside.

A dozen or so people were mingling in the town arc, talking loudly. We wouldn't have to leave after all, was their gist. Before I allowed myself to rejoice with them, there was something I wanted to see about and I set out north.

I knocked on Mud Daisy Steve's door and it wasn't answered. I found him out in the center of his flowers within a big flower, squatting. As I got near, he was whispering something to himself then started when he felt my presence.

'Steve?'

'I don't know what to do now.'

He turned and looked at me and took a defensive stance.

'Steve, Rose had been um, different today. Not well.'

'Oh?'

'You didn't sit for a single meal at my place today. You didn't bring her a flower.'

'No …'

'Well, what's going on? Whatever it is, have you thought about her once all this live-long day? She was very weak.'

'Is she all right now?'

'Yes, she's okay. She's eaten and she's drunk a well of water. She is different in her eyes. Just like you are.'

'I'm scared, Isabel.' Mud Daisy Steve shuttered and his face wrinkled up. Then as quickly, he relaxed.

'Oh Steve,' I went to him and put my arms around him.

'I'm scared of what now, I suppose. Of what now.'

'Can I help?'

'I can't ….'

'Well, come on, I'm going to feed you. I'll bet you've been out here all day. You go in your arc house and clean up some. I'll bring you leftovers. Right away.'

'Thank you.'

I watched as he lanked himself up the two porch steps and into his house, and thought to myself that whatever these two did, I'd never seen it before.

If a butterfly fell asleep on a flower and dreamed about falling asleep on a flower, would it wake twice?

When it came time for me to settle in, I first checked on Rose. My hand on her sleeping forehead felt neither too warm nor too cold, so I pulled the quilt up to her neck, tucking her in. I was anticipating a pipe-less good sleep but when I started to lie down on Rose's bed, my hand squished when I started to pull her covers back. I felt all over the bed and it was as wet as a swamp. The quilt, sheets, and the mattress itself were fit only for a frog, or a turtle maybe.

I stripped the bedding and hung it on the ra ils of the rear porch and placed the mattress out there as well. There were several small puddles of liquid on the floor of her room so I mopped those up. When finally finished, I entered Engineer Mert's room, pulled back those covers and lay down.

The song came in the window and I gave thanks for once again being able to hear it and for the return of our water.

Dreams found me awash on the plain, flooded as far as I could see. My boat was a mattress and the water swooshed it this way, then that and this went on for a long time. Back and forth, back and forth, and yet, when I came to a rest at last, I sat on the mattress not far from where I'd begun. But it was sleep.

When morning came, I was fresh. I prepared the meals for everyone and went about my usual duties. Rose stayed in my room the entire day and when I'd take meals in to her, she'd be lying prone and looking out the window. I tried small talk, but a good part of her had gone out the window, I figured, so I let it be. Mud Daisy Steve wasn't seen all day either. Teacher Rachel, upon returning from the arc schoolhouse, asked about Rose, but I had little to tell her except that she was a little ill. Mr. Ives ate well at the table, kept pretty quiet, and said he planned to sleep for days or until his eyelids turned into slices of toast and wouldn't stay down.

Then during an early evening hour, one of the pipes first let out a horrible groan, then was joined by others in the house. Soon our sand song was unseated from its gentle tonal throne.

Teacher Rachel and I first heard it while having our sit on the front porch and not long after the noise began, Mr. Ives came out, not exactly to join us.

'Do you hear that bastardly racket again? Do you hear it? Earlier today when I sunk the wells, the stick showed the wells were up several feet. What in the name of Sam Scratch is going on here?'

We all went inside and when I turned on the kitchen tap, the water balked ,only running down in the thin stream like before. The three of us just stood looking at the piddly water, our next roller-coaster ride. After a minute, my two boarders walked off to their rooms and I to my own where Rose still lay. She was still, so I went to lie on Engineer Mert's bed, feeling like a good day must have either forgotten or hadn't learned how to end well.

I didn't sleep well that night; instead of a mattress boat taking me for a ride, the dread returned that I might have to leave on the train that had always brought us things and that prospective reversal of fortune stayed in my head until morning.

No one spoke at breakfast. When I took Rose a plate I found her in her room, standing at her easel. Her color looked good and she looked recovered from her bout. I stood next to her in a silence broken only by the pipes and the soft dipping of her brush into her palette. She then asked me about Mud Daisy Steve.

I told her he hadn't been coming over here for meals and that the last time I saw him he was shaken. She nodded her head and went about her painting, and I went about my boarding house duties that I wasn't sure would be needed for long.

It was a day of side glances and not much to say. I put Rose's bed back together, clean and dry, and I continued to take meals to her. That's all I saw of her until she greeted Teacher Rachel and me out on the porch. She talked for a short time and then without goodbyes or explanation, she walked down off the porch and to the north.

The following morning, with breakfast tray in hand, I found her door open and her bed empty. When I returned to the kitchen, the others were finished and gone and I sat down. The water pipes were something I knew I couldn't get used to and I began to think that the old house didn't want us anymore.

As I sat there, I began to focus on Rose. Here came this little beauty who paints with beauty and all we're able to show her is our town falling apart. Then my curiosity came to toes with my concern and I got up and started walking toward Mud Daisy Steve's arc house.

Arrived there, I didn't knock on the door and instead walked about the side. In the bright, hot sunlight, was Rose, directly in the center of the whole flowerbed, sitting on that large disc looking like a butterfly taking a nap on a flower. I walked a tiled path and came to a shaken visage of her. She was trembling and again pale. I said her name softly and she turned to look at me.

'May I have some water?'

'Yes. Are you thirsty like befor—'

'Please.'

I walked into Mud Daisy Steve's arc house and saw him leaning up against a wall, looking somewhere over my head as if I were ten feet tall. I walked past the zombie to his kitchen and took water out to Rose.

Rose gulped the water and asked for more.

'Come with me, Rose.'

I lifted her up by one arm and steered her off the large disc, down the tiles, and into the arc house. I lay her down on a sofa and took her more water. Again she drank. I looked up at Mud Daisy Steve but he wasn't much there. Figuring that they hadn't been eating, I stole to the boarding house and returned with plates of food.

I poured water into Rose and helped her spoon some of the food into her mouth. Her eyes had that glow again and I asked her what happened.

Silence.

'Steve, what happened?' I asked him.

'I can … can't.'

Suddenly I noticed that the pipes were gradually getting quiet unlike last time when they stopped suddenly.

'Do you hear?'

'What?' Mud Daisy Larry said.

'The pipes in here, they're all quiet now.' I ran to the kitchen and turned on the faucet. Water gushed out.

'The pipes are quiet! The water is back again!'

I ran from the house and upon reaching mine, I bolted to

the kitchen whose faucet also gushed when I turned it. And the pipes were mute.

Teacher Rachel and Mr. Ives appeared in the hallway of life, both smiling. We all went outside, even Mr. Ives into the bright sunlight. Before we had a chance to comment on the song, the earth began to move beneath our feet like it had before when I watched it out the window. Gentle waves that though they didn't threaten to topple us, rattled our nerves some.

'Mr. Ives, will you check the wells?'

'In the daytime?'

'Yes. I'll get a scarf to put over you and I'll go with you.'

'A big scarf?'

'Yes, a big scarf.'

'All right.'

We found that the well was again deeper.

On the way back to the boarding house, I asked Mr. Ives about the ground rumbling. He said that there was no goddamned fault line for a thousand miles, and that no inland water table known to God or the damned devil could move the ground like that.

I left it at that.

Later I walked back to Mud Daisy Steve's, where I found that Mud Daisy Steve had pulled a chair up to the sofa, and he sat there putting water to Rose's lips. I noticed that they hadn't eaten the food, so I heated it up and sat it next to them. I left them at that, too.

slept well that night until it started up again, the banging of the dry pipes bouncing my eyelids open. Down again? I wondered if it was going to be all right here or not. I lay for a short while hoping it would stop but it didn't. I went directly to the bathroom faucet and found the same old trickle.

That day we drank and bathed and I cooked from the trickles and the more than half empty vats. A day of little event and less talk. When evening came, I told Teacher Rachel I'd skip the porch.

In my room I caught up some on this journal until I saw Rose in the hallway. Before she let herself into her room, from my doorway I asked if she was well. She said she was feeling better and asked if she could find herself some food in the kitchen. I went to her and brought her by the hand back to my room, sat her on the bed and went to the kitchen.

After she'd eaten, I fetched a brush from her room. She moved to the sway of the brush as I looked at the smooth skin covering her small bones. I thought about her being this halfway person. She had no hostility in her existing half, nothing at all to fear or feel leery about, yet there was something strong in her; maybe that is her mystery.

'Is the water back, here?' she asked.

'No, Rose, it's gone again. I'm beginning to wonder if it's the last vestiges from down there, when it flows well, or what?'

'The pipes at Mud Daisy Steve's are noisy again.'

'Yes, I suppose they are. It's all over town. I don't know how we're supposed to sleep.'

After we'd parted for an hour or two, I heard Mud Daisy Steve walk down the hallway of life. Couldn't expect him to sleep either. Probably no one is. I stayed wide awake thinking into the night about the times of the town, its setting, the leavings and returns, the deaths, the essence of the place, which as I saw it was the carrying on the heritage of our part of West Texas. Settled. People had been here long enough to stay and not know why and I thought that that was the mark of a real place, a place that held people, trains or no trains.

When I woke the next day it was already hot. I l ooked to the bed stand clock and saw that it was nearly noon. My tenants, friends, must be hungry. I washed and dressed quickly and went to the kitchen to find Teacher Rachel and Mr. Ives eating away and toasting with glasses of water. And then I realized the house was clank quiet. I asked them when the noise stopped and Mr. Ives said the great event occurred at 5:55 a.m. on the dot.

'Has Rose been out?'

'No.'

'Has Indian Jon been around?'

'No. But Mud Daisy Steve was here.'

'Oh?'

'Yes, he grabbed a bite full and left.'

'Did he say anything?'

'No, he just stared somewhere and left.'

Teacher Rachel excused herself saying that maybe she'd walk around town this fine Saturday and see what water-rejoicing the people were mustering up. Mr. Ives went to his room.

I walked down to the room in which, as I'd begun to think of her, Miss Mystery lived. Again she was pale and weak, propped up on her pillows and drinking from a glass of water.

'Can I get you something, dear?'

'No, I'm fine, Isabel. Pretty fine at least.'

'Are you hungry?'

'No, thirsty.'

I refilled her glass and noticed that her bed was again sopped. I pretended it wasn't and sat down on the edge. She seemed so comfortable in my presence, more so than usual. She was so at ease, as if she were looking at herself when she looked at me, which she did and did.

'Rose, what are you thinking?'

'I'm … I'm not, I guess. I can't think now. It's like feelings have taken over me. I lie back or prop up … anything, and I only feel like I'm wide open to air. No, not air, to, um … I don't know. To something.'

'Well, those are pretty good thoughts, Miss Unthinker.'

She giggled at that and as our eyes locked, I felt as if we were both a little taken away at thinking about feelings and feeling thoughts.

'Rose?'

'Yes?'

'You've been—'

'Isabel, I am in heavy need but maybe not in the position to have someone's ear. Something's happened and I haven't discussed it with anyone.'

'Do you think you need to?'

'I do. It's so … so … I don't know what to make of it.'

'Well, I'm aware that something's happened. Or happening. Can you talk about it with Mud Daisy Steve. He after all is—'

'Oh no, after it happens he grows quiet. Then he goes off somewhere.'

'You two are on a roller coaster of some kind.'

'Well, then it's raining on it.'

'What do you mean?'

'Isabel, when it happens, I …'

'What?'

'I flood all over.'

'Flood?'

'Look.' She patted her hand on the wet bedding.

'Like before. I see.'

She bowed her head in embarrassment and I felt some myself, this not being a topic I was used to.

'You've noticed how much water I drink after—'

'Of course I have. And you get delirious and weak.'

'The first time, I thought I was going to die. Thank you, Isabel, for looking after me.'

'That's all right.'

'When it happened again, I wasn't quite as effected but it was another large event. This last time, well, now I have needed a lot of water again and I do feel different, but I don't feel like dying or anything like that.'

'Rose?'

'Isabel, Mud Daisy Steve was right about the circles. He was right. At first I thought that he was so wrapped up in his flowers that he sort of … projected them and their ways onto me. Circles and me. Poor gentle flower man, I thought, he probably projects them onto everything and he did tell me that there is little in his life except the flowers.'

'It's been that way for twenty years.'

'Yes, I know. But he was right. The flowers showed the way for him and I can see that he's brought that way to me. It was true.'

'I'm a little lost.'

'Oh, please, Isabel, let me say this. He told me that when those ray petals on his daisies came to full circle "She loves me's ," then the central disc petals, as he calls them, rounded off their edges to such smoothness that he measured them down to a perfect 360 degree, a perfect pi.'

'H—'

'Yes, I know, I'm not a mathematician either. But then he told me that he felt that when anything in nature was full of love, or the expression of it, it was fully round. I started thinking about that and about what I see in the mirror—old Miss Halfway.'

'I—'

'It had been that way all my life. At least that's how I tended, or rather, preferred to see it.'

'Do you love him?'

'Love Mud Daisy Steve?'

She raised her head and looked away thinking, or feeling, as she'd said. She looked at me and shook her head, but not up and down for yes or side to side for no. She was moving it at an angle between the two and it looked like she was slicing them both at 45-degree angles. Cutting up two opposites. I thought, what does this mean and what could come of cutting up two things that were so ... unmeetable anyway. I'd never seen a head move like that before.

I was roused from this pondering by the first clank of a pipe in her bathroom, then more. I left Rose in silence, her head still moving at that odd angle.

'I've lived in this boarding house, like I said, most of my life and there is a lot I don't know about. I don't know about love, about men and women much, or about the ways of the world. But I know something about boarding houses. I've seen times when a boarder won't come out of his or her room for days, a week even. Yet, it is somehow known by me, by others in the boarding house, and by people in the town who haven't been in here in months or a year, what that solitary boarder has been doing, listening to on a hi-fi, reading, thinking, any and everything he's been doing. Papa called it 'stuff over the transom.' And I think I understand what he meant. But what occurred next here in Hope Pass lent to this understanding that if there is an over the transom, then there must be a through and under the transom as well.'

When Mr. Ives, unable to sleep, came to my door, I was dwelling on the things Rose had said. If not love, then is the reaction she and Mud Daisy Steve had to their activities normal? I didn't know. I'd never been in love, really. Maybe their way is the way it is all over the world out there.

'Mr. Ives, what do you know about love?'

He sat cross-legged in Mama's rocker, hand on his beard and said, "I know very little. Very little, indeed. I thought I knew it once but it went away. So it couldn't be called love. Love should be one of those rare things that stay. Mine didn't. When the object of my fake love took hers away, mine was sucked up in its exit draft, leaving nothing of it left in either party. To be polite, instead of saying that it was fake, one could perhaps call it temporary or passing love. Again, I say if one wanted to be polite. Myself, if you'll excuse me, I'd improve on the direction of fake and call that kind of love the bright shining light that shows the way to the most vacant, rat-infested dungeon of the hellhole of hell. Why, are you in love?'

'No, not me.'

'I figured it was Rose and Mud Daisy Steve. I figure whatever kind of love it is or isn't, it came quite quickly upon them.'

We heard people coming down the hallway of life and soon saw Teacher Rachel and others lined up outside my door.

'Isabel, I've been on the porch. I was approached by these others and we have something to say.'

Into the room came Teacher Rachel, Constable Betsy, Mr. and Mrs. Blass, the nearest neighbors, and Mr. O'Connell, our resident snakeologist who'd always come running whenever a rattler was spotted in town and who'd always capture it and return it to the desert sands.

'What is it, Rachel?'

'Isabel, this may sound crazy to you but we all feel the same.'

'About what?'

'The pipes, the water, Rose and Mud Daisy Steve.'

'What about them Rachel, what is it?'

'We think that when Rose and Mud Daisy Steve get together the water rises.'

'What?'

'We do.'

'I'm a—'

'Isabel. Mr. Blass—in fact, about everyone has noticed. Look, this is a small place. He's seen the sand out on the plain move just after those two have—'

'Mr. Blass,' I said, 'are you watching their movements?'

'Of course I am. We all are. We figured it out. They're together, the water rises, the pipes shut up. They're apart, the water sinks and we have that racket.'

'You mean to tell me that you all believe what they do raises the water?'

'We do,' said Constable Betsy.

'Well, I think you've all lost your—'

'Wait a minute, Isabel,' interrupted Mr. Ives, 'they may have something there.'

'Mr. Ives!'

'Let them finish.'

'Since this—since they started, the pipes stop and the water runs for a while. Then after a short time, back to the noise and trickles from our faucets. Think of how it's happened,' said Teacher Rachel.

'I can't believe it,' I said.

'It is deductive,' said Mr. Ives.

'Mr. Ives, I could use a sane hand here.'

'It's an interesting proposition, I must say. It could be proven or disproven,' he said.

'Oh? How?'

'Get them together,' said Mr. Blass.

'Get Rose and Mud Daisy Larry together and see if they can make the stupid pipes be quiet?'

'Well,' said Constable Betsy, 'they do like each other's company. That's plain to see.'

'So, should I go ask them to spend time together? Just like that? Right now?'

'Why not?' asked the snakecatcher.

'What if they don't *want* to spend time together?'

'You could coax them.'

'Like you do your snakes?'

'That's not fair.'

Constable Betsy, strategist that she was, came then with, 'Isabel, we all live together here, look out for one another. It would do a lot of good, if we're right, to persuade Rose to be with Mud Daisy Steve so they could possibly save our town.'

'You're asking me to pander her. Pander both of them!'

As my voice rose, so did my eyes and I saw Rose standing outside the doorway behind the others. Our eyes met and then she quickly vanished.

The pall cast, there was nothing under it left to be said. Everyone left the room and I was left to consider the strange workings of transoms, full circles, deduction and, oh yes, sources of water.

closed my door and lay deep in the bed thinking, how could they believe this? What does Rose think of us now? One for all but not all for one was their request. Poor Teacher Rachel, to have been a part of it. Maybe her connection with her students connects her to families like I'm not.

I crawled out of bed and walked to Rose's room. It was a timid rap on her door but she heard it.

'Isabel?'

She silently stood aside to let me in and I walked straight to her dresser and picked up one of her brushes. She was still quiet as her head swayed side-to-side, swaying as I stroked her threads. Finally, I spoke to her.

'Rose, do you forgive us?'

Nothing.

'How much did you hear?'

'I got the gist of it.'

'I'm so sorry.'

'Yea. But it wasn't you, Isabel, I heard what you said.'

'I don't know what came over them.'

'Ah, maybe they're right.'

'What? What are you saying?'

'Not about coaxing me and Mud Daisy Steve. But about the pipes and water.'

'How can you say that?'

'Well … you know that I haven't been much aware of things afterward, or during … And if that many people think there's a connection, even Teacher Rachel, then …'

'But how could it be?'

'I don't know.'

'Well, you and Mud Daisy Steve aren't going to join because others want you to. Not for water pipes or anything. It's ghastly.'

'No, we won't do that. I won't do that.'

'Well, if anyone tells you that you should, come to me. I'll see about—'

'No. If they ask, I'll tell them myself. I am beginning to think they're right, though.'

'I've never heard of such a thing,'

'Me either, Isabel.'

'Then why now? Here?'

'Maybe it is the circling.'

'The cir— Oh, Mud Daisy Steve's—'

'His proof on that count.'

Fewer people worked their arc booths the next morning and word was in the air that couples were trying to quiet pipes and raise water levels without Rose and Mud Daisy Steve's help. But in time the arc booths became as people—stocked as usual, the pipes hadn't shut up nor had the faucets opened up.

When Teacher Rachel returned from her lesson-giving, I met her at the door to the boarding house and asked her if she'd reconsidered her ideas concerning Rose and Mud Daisy Steve and pipes and water.

'No. I don't pretend to understand all the workings of nature, Isabel, but quite a few people noticed the coordination of their activity and the water levels and they say the whole plain out there rolls about after they've met.'

'You don't believe it's only wishful thinking?'

'No, and I'll tell you another reason why. Those people and

you, me, and all of us live only here, in our isolated place. Without more water, all are faced with leaving. Leaving our home. Their home. So I think, all-important as that is, they are keen to things concerning such a drastic change. Watching things. Yes, I believe so. They think these events are married and so do I.'

'Teacher Rachel, you've always been so brilliant. You and Mr. Ives soar above us all in that. And now you're saying that magic of some sort is occurring here. Think of it.'

'I have. Over and over. Constantly now, really. Just listen to those pipes.' And she swung an arm in a motion that was meant to cover the entire boarding house. 'Have those two been together today?'

'No, he's not been here.'

'Doesn't that say something?'

'God, I can't bring myself to believe it.'

'What could be another explanation?'

"I don't know but have you heard the talk about others trying it?'

'What?'

'People are ... coming together again to try to foster what they think Rose and Mud Daisy Steve caused.'

'Really, Isabel?'

"It's the rumor.'

'I'll be. It didn't work.'

'See?'

Mud Daisy Steve was absent from the table that night so when the meal was finished and after Mr. Ives and Rose had gone to their rooms, I suggested to Teacher Rachel that we forego our porch sit.

'Alright.'

'But come, come with me.'

'Where?'

'Just come.'

We walked to Rose's room and both sat on the edge of her bed facing her.

'Rose, I'm not one in the habit of creating or perpetuating ill. Heck, how could I be? There's little opportunity for it here anyway.'

'I know that, Rachel, I can tell,' responded Rose while she looked straight into the teacher's eyes.

'Rose,' I said, 'Rachel believes what the others do but I've known her well and I know she didn't mean to offend you.'

'It's forgotten. And as I told you, their belief may be mine as well.'

'Did you know that others in town were trying it today to bring the water and make the pipes be quiet,' I said.

'Others?'

'I guess so.'

'It must not have worked,' said Rose, 'the pipes are loud.'

'So maybe there goes the connection,' I said.

'Maybe,' she responded.

'Well, that clears the air some,' I said.

'I wonder what if ...'

'What, Rose?'

'I wonder if Mud Daisy Steve's circling ...' Rose put her hand up to her mouth as to bar escape and blushed.

'Circling?' asked Teacher Rachel. 'Isabel ...'

'I can't.'

'Maybe I can,' enjoined Rose, 'maybe I should. We're all women, after all.'

'What is circling, then?' asked Teacher Rachel.

'Don't tell anyone. Don't tell Mud Daisy Steve I said this.'

'We won't,' I vowed, and then recalled the power and the various methods of things to escape the transom.

'Mud Daisy Steve bred the perfect flower and says this perfection came to represent to him the potential for anything, everything to be perfect.'

'Go on.'

'Teacher Rachel, after only one failed attempt, we closed on one another in an openness that went full. He asked me if I would open up my whole being for him. This isn't easy to talk about.'

'Please—' pleaded Teacher Rachel.

'So, it happened the second time.'

'What?'

'I opened to a full wide circle. Like his flowers.'

'Then what?'

'Everything let go ... out of me. And I had to be refreshed afterward. I was able to let everything go for the first time in my life, I believe.'

'Everything?'

'I think everything, Rachel.'

Rose continued: 'Once when I'd said I was the "Halfway Girl" to Mud Daisy Steve, he said "So far." I asked him what he meant and he said he'd been watching me and could see there was something to it. Then he said it was that way with his daisies when he began with them. But they opened into perfection in words and deeds—the "Loves me's and the circle, perfect pi." He said I could do the same thing.'

'Geez. Geez,' sputtered Teacher Rachel.

'That's what he said. I thought about it for a couple of days and then I told him I was willing to try.'

'Yes?'

'It didn't work. It was … a failed experiment, I guess.'

'Well, then what?'

'We tried again and I … well, I must have circled.'

'What was it like?'

'Like the whole earth ran out of me, like I was the earth. Like because I was so wide open, open as any woman ever, maybe, nothing could be held back.'

I looked over at Rachel and her dark skin reddened and mine must have too.

'Anything else, Rose?'

'Only that I disappeared into something when I began to gush, a flooding out of me that floated me away also.'

She said that when it was over she felt like a solid lump with no lubrication or liquid anywhere in her body. At least until she'd recovered with water and time as a little different person than before.

'How so?'

'I've seen something, I believe, been something new from before. I didn't want to be halfway anymore. That's why we did this again … and again.'

'Was it the same?' asked Teacher Rachel.

'The second time. The third time it felt more natural. Still all gone different and I again felt complete but more natural-like.'

I didn't know what Teacher Rachel made of all this once she went to her room late that night but I know that I kept company in my own room with not only the pipes' squawk, but also with a blurry picture of a woman, any woman, spread to the world and getting the whole world in return.

My third day in Hope Pass was coming to an end and I began to doubt some of Aunt Isabel's words. The circling business began to look like some sort of literary shot aimed at a dresser drawer, wrapped in the cloak of a leather journal left for what reason now.

With only a week to go until the train would pass and back up, and with enough faucet trickle and vat water to see us through, box hopes rose back up to their prominent places in peoples' minds. We were all weary of the noisy pipes and the mystery of things going up and back down but this didn't slay the general monthly expectation. As for me, I saw it as a dual to be held on the platform boards between a fine new cardboard box to be opened on them and this Rose leaving us by stepping off them.

I became aware that Rose had packed some other things and had collapsed her easel. I asked her to come to my room and I led her to an open window. I pointed to the northeast where we could see the distant train tracks that set themselves as the sole player on the stage of bright sands. I said I wouldn't try to talk her out of leaving but that I'd look out this window in the future and be able to see that her crossing those sands made them brighter yet. I thanked her for her friendship and for bringing us something above what we'd known. She demurred but I felt I couldn't let her go without a testament to her, a compliment of action.

I told her that we all might be leaving in months or a year and that if that happened I would look for her wherever I ended up. She said she'd look up from whatever life was to hold for her and try to see me too. She said that the portrait she'd done of me was one of her best ever.

We both turned to the wall where it hung and she said that my eyes are the best eyes she'd ever painted and that the film wasn't thick or deep.

'It is real though, Isabel, but I don't think it runs to your soul.'

Before she left my room, she said I'd been like an older sister to her for the short time she'd been here and she'd carry that with her.

I interrupted a chore probably a half dozen times that day to return to my room and study my eyes, sometimes pulling the shawl photograph out again to compare those eyes. I tried to see how deep that film went and what was beneath it and what wasn't.

In the evening, I decided to once again forego my porch time with Teacher Rachel and walk around Hope Pass. On the porch, I found her and a rare sight, Mr. Ives, talking about their lack of sleep. I started south and decided to go to the rear of the boarding house where Indian Jon's tepee stood.

I stood at the flap door and said 'knock, knock,' and the voice from inside said, 'Who's there—come in.'

Indian Jon was sitting by his fire looking straight into it.

'Indian Jon?'

'Yea?'

'What do you think of me?'

'You're a good woman. Not an Awoik woman but a good woman.'

'What do you see in my eyes?'

'Same thing as in all of us, all of you here and me.'

I sat down across the fire from him and looked at his eyes. They are very dark and I saw that they didn't sparkle. They looked out from a deep, solid place, I thought.

'Why do we have it?'

'I don't say about yours, Isabel. I've had mine these years since I left my people, my other people.'

He handed me his pipe and I smoked with him and became quiet and saddened. He would look up from the fire and, film-to-film, we'd stared, then he'd look back at the flames.

I asked him what he thought about the water and pipes changing like they had and he said he'd heard the talk. I immediately gained even more respect for the transom, for it obviously could turn corners and go about anywhere it chose, even in through the hide of or a hole in a tepee.

'Do you believe it?'

'I've never felt the Great Mother move like it did.'

'You felt it too?'

'Yea, she moved under my tepee.'

'Is she pleased?'

"I think so.'

'Rose is leaving.'

'I figured.'

'How?'

'Isabel, woman, I am not holy or old but I have been practicing Awoik medicine for years now. I do know some things.'

'Will the water rise and the ground quiver after Rose leaves?'

'No.'

'I'm scared, Indian Jon. I'm scared that the water will be gone soon. I'm afraid to leave here.'

He rose amid the bustle of the deerskins he wore and came to sit next to me. He said that he didn't know about the water's direction but that it would not remain the same.

I placed my head on his shoulder and he placed his arm around me. I wasn't used to being touched and the warmth of it was soft and it moved past where his hand rested. We sat like that for quite some time and then he got to his feet and walked past the dwindling fire to where his bedding lay.

'You stay here tonight, Isabel.'

I walked over to him and he held me with both arms. Then they were out into the first light of day or shadow of night, except for inside my room, in twenty years. The smoky air treated my breasts well and they somehow thanked me for this freedom.

'Am I old, Indian Jon?'

'You're like me. Forty-five and forty-five to go.'

When I first felt the blanket, I remember thinking about what Rose had said and then I lost thought and looked up into the hole at the top of the tepee where the top of the poles exited into the night. There was moonlight coming in and I watched it as I opened. Wide, then wider, until I felt my parts meet other parts of me. I felt like I was open to the world, spread for everything and that's when we met and fit.

I felt as if the whole inside of my being was expanding, bloating, and then it released and ran a flood from out of the meeting place. A tap was opened full, of a sudden and then more, and then a great wash and I was empty, leaving only Indian Jon and t he banks of the river down there. I shook and quivered and wept from dry eyes.

I awoke to the touch of water on my lips, which felt parched, deserty. He gave me water until the ground under us moved in a long rolling wave that lifted everything in the tepee and then set all back down a little ways away from where things had stood.

He walked me around to the boardinghouse, at what night hour I don't know. We parted inside the front doors and when I got to my room, I could hear there was quiet, all except for the song that could be heard singing itself in through the windows. I slept.

I took the journal with me and walked to the rear of the house. There I kicked around and found old burned pieces of wood under the sands. Deeper there were signs that a number of fires had burned there, one on top of the other. I sat down under the blaze above this desert and rolled one of the pieces of wood round and round between two fingers. Circles. Circles and wide openings took place here, so she says. Then why had they gone, if water could be made to rise in their wells?

could make out Rose and Teacher Rachel at my bedside. They looked clearer. When Teacher Rachel's hand brought a water glass to my lips I could see the ridges on her fingernails and the darker skin that covered her knuckles. They were beautiful hands, the first time I'd truly looked at them.

'How do you feel, Isabel?'

'I don't know—different.'

'Isabel, the pipes stopped last night and water is flowing again.'

I could hear Mr. Ives' footfalls as he approached. He said that whatever happened to Rose and me—there's that transom again—he'd like to see it continue so the noise would stay away and the water would run so we can all stay in Hope Pass.

'To say nothing of the sand song. I'm going back to my room and sleep. It's good to see you well, Isabel.'

I slowly let go of my vagueness but I watched closely and my vision stayed most clear. Rose was staring at my eyes.

'Isabel, you've been someplace.'

'Yes, Rose, I guess I have.' I reached out my hands to her and she laid her head on my shoulder. I then reached for Teacher Rachel and she rested on my other shoulder.

'Everyone found out,' Rose said.

'Everyone?'

'Yes. Quite a troop came in to look at you.'

'Has Indian Jon been here?'

'He came in once and stood cross-armed over you. He didn't say a word, only looked and looked at you.'

That's the last I remember until waking to the piping. I swore that if we ever got them to quiet forever, we'd be just as forever loud in our praise of the sand song.

I made it to the kitchen late at night and saw that my boarders had managed well. I ate what Teacher Rachel had cooked and sat at the table with a lit candle. Still later, Indian Jon came in the door and said he'd like to sleep in his room in the boarding house that night.

He sat across from me at the table and as I looked at him, his eyes didn't look as dark as the night before. Neither of us said a word for moments and moments and then he rose from his chair and began walking back to his room.

'The noise is back, Indian Jon.'

'I still want to sleep in here tonight.'

The following dawn came slow, dragging sleepy people out of tosses and turns. After breakfast, when Teacher Rachel went to her school and Mr. Ives to his room, I sought out Rose.

She was as giddy as I'd seen her, prancing about her room and then she'd stand suddenly still and toss things into an open suitcase clear across the room from her. Her easel was back up.

'What's gotten in to you, dearie?'

'Oh, Isabel, I'm a flower. The more I've been thinking about those mud daisies, the more I feel like I'm one of them.'

'Maybe you are.'

'Maybe you are, too.' And she giggled and threw her hair back.

'Me?'

'You made the circle, didn't you?'

'I believe so.'

'You must feel like I do—no more half-way Rose.'

She continued to have more fun packing then anyone I'd ever seen. She'd toss stockings in her suitcase, helter-skelter, even her hairbrushes were thrown. I thought then that maybe she truly did think she was a flower. It occurred to me then that maybe those mud daisies were the only things that were whole, and maybe wholesome around here for years. When I said this to Rose she said she'd not been here for those years to bear witness to that. She said that yes, the flowers were whole, and so was she and me also, she felt.

She said she wanted to touch up my portrait, the eyes, and that she'd return it that very day.

While I was still in her room, Constable Betsy, Mr. O'Connell, and a few other townspeople appeared at her open door.

'We've heard what happened,' said Constable Betsy. 'We'd like one of you ... to quiet the pipes and make the—'

'It's not like that,' I said, 'and besides, we've been through this before.'

'We've heard about the circling activity.'

'How?'

'Just heard, that's all.'

'Then why don't you try it, Constable Betsy,' I said.

'Me? Me? Why ... I never ...'

'And what about you, Mr. and Mrs. Blass, why don't you try it?'

They both dropped their eyes and some of my anger left me.

'We've tried. But circles?'

'Circles," I said.

There was a moment or two of hemming and hawing and then they left, freeing Rose and I from becoming water prostitutes, I guess.

Later in the day as Rose was hanging the shiny-eyed

portrait back on its nail in my room, she abruptly turned to me and I looked back at her smile. The pipes ha d suddenly gone mute. I went to the faucet and it flowed just like after Rose and I had run as rivers.

'They did it!' she said.

'We're off the forced hook,' I responded.

planned a celebration for Rose, in gratitude for my portrait and more so for what she'd brought to us: her beauty for a while and that other.

Teacher Rachel and Mr. Ives helped with the preparations and they spread the word around town. Mud Daisy Steve said he'd pick a posy of his best. I went to the rear of the boarding house to tell Indian Jon and he returned to the kitchen with me.

When all was made ready, there at the table with the hairbrush-shaped cake I'd baked sat only the Indian. We waited for a long time and no one came either from their rooms off the hall of life or from the town. I went to Rose's room first and she wasn't there. Teacher Rachel's door was wide open but she was out too. I then knocked on Mr. Ives' door and heard muffled sounds louder than the pipes. I knocked a second time and heard a splashing sound.

I returned to the kitchen and told Indian Jon that it looked like we'd be eating alone. As I poured water for us the water whooshed out of the tap, jumping in a wide gush that soaked the counter and the front of my clothing. I lunged to turn it off but the gush wouldn't obey the faucet handle. The Indian jumped up and put his strength to it but it did no good. I told him about the main shut off to the house and he ran out the door, headed to the rear of the house.

'It's broken off.'

'What?'

'Look!' he said, pointing down the hall of life.

'What on earth!' I could see a small stream of water running out from under my door. Inside, the bathroom faucet was also running wild. It wouldn't shut off. Down the hall of life, Rose's room was getting wet as was Teacher Rachel's. I sped to Mr. Ives' door and knocked loudly, then screamed for him to open up.

Mr. Ives opened the door, saying, 'She's flooded.'

'Is your tap running fast?'

He didn't respond and walked right past Indian Jon and me. We watched him as he walked out the boarding house door.

I looked at Indian Jon, shrugged my shoulders, and went into the room to behold Teacher Rachel lying on her back with her arms extended over her head and her hands against the headboard trying to push herself toward the foot of the bed. But she wasn't moving. The bed was soaked. I went to the door and told Indian Jon that Teacher Rachel wasn't decent and then I returned to her. I'd never once seen her complete blackness before and I caught myself staring at the contrast between her and the white, wet sheet beneath her.

'Rachel? Rachel?'

She looked up at me so expressionless as to express a lot or everything, I remember thinking.

'Water.'

I turned to the faucet and saw that that sink was overflowing. That tap didn't work either.

I gave Rachel water and before I covered her, I saw flakings of lighter skin on hers and small splotches of what I figured were oozings from Mr. Ives. I filled another glass and she took to it avidly.

I beckoned to Indian Jon.

'What are we going to do?'

'I don't know. None of them turn off.'

'It will ruin everything.'

Indian Jon turned and ran out of the room while I gave Teacher Rachel more water. I turned to see that her faucet was still gushing and the water was getting deeper. This had never happened before here—too much water had never been one of our concerns. It just kept running.

After a couple of minutes, Indian Jon returned and said that the well out back was rising up its walls.

'Are they all doing that?'

'I can go see.'

By the time he returned, I was standing ankle deep in the stuff.

'What's happening?' I shouted, as panic arrived.

'It's everywhere. They're all coming up.'

'Are arc houses getting wet?'

'Some.'

'What are they doing about it?'

'Little.'

'Little?'

'They open their door and they look like Teacher Rachel there looks.'

'Indian Jon?'

'They don't act like they care.'

'Christ Sakes!'

Teacher Rachel then moved under the cover I'd placed over her and brought her hands down to her sides.

'I was the circle.'

'Rachel?'

'I made the circle.'

I looked straight at her, at the soggy bedding and realized that, yes, that must have happened. My thoughts then ran quickly to my ankles.

Indian Jon left, returned, and said that all the floors were getting very wet. We looked at each other helplessly.

Then I asked him to help me open all the windows in the boarding house as wide as they'd go. And the front doors. I retrieved every bucket and we began bailing out the front door.

We could see that this did little good. I tossed down a bucket and looked around at the front entryway. The legs on the table were deep in it. I flit to my room and placed a favored basket and a pair of shoes on top of my bed. Then the wooden music stand Papa had given me. I waded to Rose's room and put her easel on her bed, to Teacher Rachel 's, where I put small things on hers, and in Mr. Ives' room I lifted books and placed them on his dresser.

'We're going to have to get Teacher Rachel out of here if this continues.'

I sloshed out of Mr. Ives room and headed for the door in search of help. Mr. Ives was standing at the side of the porch, looking like he was incapable of doing anything. Next door I found Mr. Blass languidly hauling possessions out of his arc house. He neither nodded nor spoke to me.

'Where is Mrs. Blass?'

'In bed.'

I entered the arc house and found this woman acting like Teacher Rachel was acting.

'Water …"

I gave her some water.

'Mrs. Blass, you need to help your husband. Your things will be ruined.' I gave her more water and left to walk on to other arc houses. Many had water running out of them and in some yards stood large and small pieces of furniture.

'Rose?' I walked briskly in the other direction, past the boarding house where Indian Jon was tying Bow and Arrow to the top of the porch and where Mr. Ives was still standing blank. When I arrived at Mud Daisy Steve's arc house, water poured from there. He was standing still, looking off somewhere again and Rose was again lying on the sofa drinking water and apparently oblivious to the fact that more of it was on the floor and getting deeper by the minute.

'Wake up, you two!'

They were jolted to it some and I told them we needed to do something.

'What?' said Mud Daisy Steve.

'Well, man, you invented a flower, maybe you can invent something now.'

'What?'

'I don't know.'

I brought Rose to her feet and asked her to help me take things outside. Mud Daisy Steve sparked up enough to place flowers and packets of seeds on the top of bookcases and counters.

When we were finished with what we could lift and with what Mud Daisy Steve loved, we walked hurriedly to my house and with Indian Jon's help, did the same thing with everyone's favorite belongings in there.

Afterward, we stood in the yard watching the liquid wash out the door and launch itself off the porch to the yard. Indian Jon pointed toward the side of the house and we could see a small rivulet of water coming from the rear. We ran through this water and at the rear we saw that water was bubbling up out of the well, its sweep and bucket ballasted by the surge and swinging back and forth to the bubbling.

The tepee was now sitting in a pool and Indian Jon ran inside it. He tossed out to us his beaded moccasins, prayer bags, and then he emerged with his chanupa to smoke another day.

'Look,' said Rose, pointing to the Blass well, 'I wonder if they're all like that.'

'They must be,' said Mr. Ives. He then took off at a pretty good pace and returned a minute later, dragging a long ladder.

'Yea, yea,' said Indian Jon.

I looked at them and then at Rose. I asked him to put it up in the front of the house and Rose and I waded in and dressed Teacher Rachel. It took all five of us to lift her and take her outside. We propped her up in a high lawn chair and went next door. We carried Mrs. Blass out and set her up comfortably in her front yard. And so, three of us went from arc house to arc house to the south and Indian Jon and Mr. Ives went north, helping those women who couldn't get out or get help from their husbands. Children helped and when we got to Constable Betsy's arc house, we needed them. For though we found Mr. O'Connell inside, we found our Constable stuffed full of and surrounded by inertia. We lugged her out, noting that the package in the bright flowery dress seemed to weight near what five people would. Mr. O'Connell was led out by the merest tug on his sleeve.

The water was now knee high in the houses and nearing the ankle out in the yards. The first voiced suggestion of what we should do—camp out way out in the plain— was nixed after Indian Jon and Bow and Arrow returned from a short reconnoiter to announce that the water had headed out in all four directions and that we'd have to carry things to dry places, but those could be a long way out judging by how fast the water was moving.

So we went from house to house gathering up ladders and putting them up. As night fell, flashlights and lanterns helped guide our few children and plodding women up to the roofs of their arc houses.

By midnight, the townspeople were all aloft on the flat roofs of their houses and food and blankets had been taken up. At near dawn, my boarders and Mud Daisy Steve and Indian Jon lay blankets across the roof of the boarding house. Before we lay down our weary heads, we peaked over the edge of the roof and could see that the wells were still bubbling up over their rims and that water was over two feet deep in the yards.

So tired. So very tired, were we. We slept in the wind and the sand song.

I carried the journal with me and took a look at the outside of the boardinghouse, that line on it and then at the lines on the arc houses. They were each about 4-5 feet high. I was able to climb a porch post and a drainpipe and peer onto the roof of the boardinghouse. There were remnants of cloth covered by sand and bleached by the sun. So, they did sleep up here, those hopers, those long gone hopers.

dreamed of being rocked slowly back and forth, the full forty-five years of me, lying on Mama's lap as she rocked in her chair. As I looked up at her she was still as young as when she had died, as if good health and comfort hadn't neglected her. I imagined that if she'd lived she would have burst with joy as she aged, instead of having been overtaken.

I woke to a swaying and looked around me to see that lumps near me, the people sleeping under their blankets were also rolling. Mud Daisy Steve was on his knees looking down over the edge of the roof. His head and shoulders went this way and that as if he were in a boat on a rough lake.

I crawled from beneath my quilt and crept over to where the grower knelt and I did likewise beside him. He looked at me, raised his eyebrows, and nodded them down to the ground. There was no ground; the water was feet deep and had waves that kicked up against the side of the boarding house. Past the yards, the plain was gone. I could see the twin peaks far off and they looked like pictures of pharos I'd seen in books. I became alarmed at the thought that we might all have to make for them if the water kept coming up or if our food ran out. I rose and crawled to the rear part of the roof and could see that where wells were there were now fountains bubbling up more and more. The image of mama's rocker returned to me out in the front of the building, where I'd last seen it, swimming among booths in an element that would rot it.

Soon the others were up and I went past them to look for the rocker but was no longer in the yard that had turned ocean. I looked out in front of me and there it was leaning up against one of the canopied booths and it was still rocking back and forth, back and forth, at an angle strangely reminiscent of the angle at which Rose had once shaken her head at a question I'd posed to her.

Mr. Ives approached me and whispered in my ear.

'Yes, you're right. All the food.'

'We should do it soon, Isabel.'

'Yes.'

We spread the word and soon we all were going down the ladder, all except Rachel, who lay back down.

The morning was spent with some of us carrying food items on top of our heads to the ladder where Mud Daisy Steve and Indian Jon took them up the ladder to our loft. We saw that the Blasses were doing the same and there was like active live on other ladders and roofs.

We ate, but found that our appetites didn't have appetite of their own. We had days' supply anyway, enough, I guessed, to get us by until the train came. If it could.

Under the blankets we'd strung so as not to fry in the sun, the usual desert winds blew in though without a drowned out or drowned sand song, which quiet we took as natural because there were no sands in sight. So we were calm in our lack of calm until it hit in the afternoon, as the plain rose up a great heave, rising us straight up and down. We landed on what later turned to bruises and then our eyes and mouths went wide again as the heave returned and again we rose and fell in plunks.

Once again the rise and fall. We all scampered toward

Teacher Rachel. Mr. Ives held her hand and we all knelt near her waiting for the next upheaval. After a few moments, a low whimpering could be heard from out on the plain. It let up for a few seconds and again it was heard as if it traveled rapidly across the breadth and width of all that was out there.

'Is it an earthquake, Mr. Ives?' asked Rose.

'Beats the hell out of me what that is; I've never heard of an earthquake acting like that.'

Indian Jon lurched to his feet and ran toward the ladder.

'Where are you going? You could be hu—' I began.

'Bow and Arrow.'

Mr. Ives walked to the rear and said that the wells were spouting like geysers, gushing feet above the already deep surface water.

'More? So much more yet?' Mud Daisy Steve said.

'Will it rise up to us? I asked.

No one answered. To anything, except the Indian to his horse. He said he tied her legs firm, for now, and then he produced his chanupa and filled it while singing an Awoik song, all the time looking up at his mountains. He sat down and smoked and we all did the same. I turned my head and looked up at those mountains and wondered if that's where we'd all end up, where his song was headed.

The next morning Mud Daisy Steve went down the ladder and retrieved more viands and pots for our other needs, and some of the ocean for us to drink and bathe in. The house rolled on a wave from the desert from time to time and once in a while a more boisterous aftershock, as we came to call them, rocked us pretty good. It was then that I looked out onto the town and saw that arc houses had been moved, turned around a bit, and the boarding house also faced more southerly.

I pointed this out to Teacher Rachel who was on her feet for the first time since her circling. When she looked about Hope Pass, at the change in the houses and all the water, she said only "I wonder how my students will learn anything way up on the rooves of their houses." And then she went to where Mr. Ives was sitting and she got near him under his blanket umbrella.

Mud Daisy Steve, looking to the north, said to no one in particular but perhaps to everyone, that he could almost see his daisies. "Underwater, yes, but they must be waving their ray petals to the end of their round and happy endings in the underwater currents flowing through their beds." He said that he should go to them so that they would know he's still about but then he signed, sat down, and looked out some more.

At midday, Indian Jon said that the wells were still funneling up a little, that the water level had stabilized, and that his teepee still stood its ground and water. Mr. Ives joined in and said that the winds take some water away with them and the dry desert air did the same. When the next tremor occurred, he watched closely and said that it caused only a short gushing and that it looked like the worst of the flooding was past. He then said, amidst our relief at his forecast, that we should go down the ladder and check the food supply and morale of other roofers. Mud Daisy Steve followed him down and they headed north, under the ooze-tormenting sunlight and Indian Jon and I went in the other direction.

We helped people get more food and found that families were joining together on selected rooftops. The people were taking the changes well. There was talk of the train's box arriving soon, so all being as well as could be expected, we waded back. Mud Daisy Steve and Mr. Ives said pretty much the same thing when they returned. I began hoping oh so dearly that the water would go away with a trailer hope coming close behind it: that the mess down below wouldn't be more than we could bear.

I decided to go down and take a good look inside my boarding house and the Indian went with me to give more attention to his horse. My kitchen was—well, un-well. Where mama had once stood and cooked I saw a brackish lake, feet deep. No one could cook in there, I thought, unless they had a small boat and an anchor to steady a dough-kneading or a soup-stirring hand. The rest of the house looked the same. I went into my room with my eyes in a protective, save-the-view misery squint. The dresser was wet two drawers up and the third had absorbed some water. I opened the top one and stared at my photograph.

I turned and saw that Indian Jon was standing at the doorway and had been watching me.

I asked him why all this water. Why ... oh why. He didn't respond in word, but took me by the hand and then with his hands on my shoulders, lowered me onto my bed, only a foot higher then the level of the water.

They were released again into the open air. Then my other was bared and we joined as my lower limbs got farther and farther away from each other and again I felt I was open to the world. It wasn't long before I felt my own river and from my pose it began to flow in swooshes and gushes of its own. I felt many things leaving me and then I was being moved all over. I looked to my side and the water was at a level with the bed. I tried to say something but couldn't.

Indian Jon stood up and pulled me to him. He led me out of the room and as we reached the hall of life a large quake struck and tossed us up against a wall. He recovered and gathered me up again. I don't remember anything that followed and woke to see Rose and Teacher Rachel kneeling over me on the roof. They were giving me water. Teacher Rachel said the wells had shot up again and the earth had been quaking and moving the house up and down a little. Rose said that the water down below was about a foot deeper than before.

As I slowly came back I realized what we'd done. What sort of strange connection this was—I didn't know. I began to fear that because others had also circled, maybe we'd never get off the rooftops unless it all ceased. I crept over to Indian Jon and told him what I thought.

'Yes. She awake now.'

'Who?'

I thought of Engineer Mert and how he described the lay of this land, the great creature that had strode and slept here. He'd said it had made this town and others.

'Indian Jon? What do you think she'll do next?'

'I believe she's been sleeping a long time. I think she will stay awake now.'

'Will the water stay?'

'Our mother. I think the drumming in my home is her heartbeat. She's been awakened.'

'You think we woke her?'

'She slept a long time.'

'Is she angry?'

'She doesn't get angry. She is the earth. She's only awake.'

'We shouldn't have—'

'No. Not anymore. Not here.'

We agreed that we'd tell our roofers what we did and that we should all go to other rooves and beseech everyone to refrain from circling.

Again I walked around to the rear of the house. But it was more the side, I now gauged. The houses had been moved some, soaked more, abandoned completely.

It was two days until the train was due and we sat on the roof in the dawning. Mr. Ives sat near me and said the buildings would rot if underwater for an extended time and that the mess inside them, if the water ever receded, would be too much for any army to clean and make right.

'Well, what would you have me do?'

'I don't know about you, Isabel, but for me, I believe I'll go if the train can make it in here.'

'Go? Go where?'

'I don't know, but go.'

'Mr. Ives, what do you truly feel is going on here?'

'I've never heard of it before. A flood from under, like this. Some sort of rare—I suppose because you asked for my true feelings, I'll give them—antigua mater phenomenon. That's all I can tell.'

'You think we caused it? Helped it?'

'Something like that.'

As our talk tailed off, a tremor was felt. Indian Jon walked to the edge of the roof and announced that the wells in sight were funneling up high again. He came to where I was sitting and reminded me that the Mother would continue as long as people in the town were coming together. He walked to the ladder and descended. I watched as he appeared on top of the Blasses' arc house. He made several arm gestures while talking to Mr. Blass and then he left. He was seen a few moments later on the roof of the arc house next down the way.

I pulled my blanket up to my chin trying, I guess, to protect myself from the dirt and grime that I knew was accumulating in the boarding house. The wind must be blowing some in to join what the water brought. 'What would Papa do?' reverberated in my head. What am I going to do? I have Mr. Ives and Teacher Rachel to care for, I whined silently. This is their home, they can't leave. It's the only home I've ever known.

Indian Jon returned some hours after he'd departed on his, oh, none-of-that mission and said that he'd asked all adults not to.

'What did they say?'

'They agreed, overall. Everyone has it figured out or think they have.'

'How are their supplies?'

'There is food to eat. Not much. A day or two's worth.'

'Their spirits?'

'They … you people have always been calm. It's a different calm now. An odd peace, maybe, though eyes are wide at this water.'

I crawled out from under my blanket and went to where Rose and Mud Daisy Steve were sitting. I told them that maybe the water would go away now that Indian Jon had succeeded in his mission. I told Mr. Ives and Teacher Rachel the same thing.

We had adapted to the roof. We had our blanket canopies, a place to ease and toss it into the ocean and there was enough food. There were many silently exchanged looks, clear looks into our blurry future.

There were no more tremors that whole day and by dusk, the well's flow was back at surface level about five feet off the ground. Before pitch and moon met I looked out onto the town arc and saw that Mama's rocker had disappeared. There was nothing in the yard but liquid, nor could I see any furniture or belongings in adjacent yards. All was washed away.

I lay down in a world of high air and deep water waves and felt that I still had many things. I counted mama and papa, my boarders, the memory of what had recently happened to me. I knew I could hold onto these people and the memories even if the boarding house decided to become a big old boat and just set sail for forever on our well-water ocean.

I again toured the town. Standing up against an arc house, I hand-leveled the watermark on it to mid-chest level. Yes, her flood had occurred. I could see the handle of a sewing basket here or the leg of a small desk there, mostly buried in sand. A large trunk laid upside down, its bottom cooked clean by years of hot moving sand.

As I neared the end of journal and near the end of my own supplies, I began to feel that I was somehow, to some degree, ending like they did. Or at least I could feel what an imminent departure from this Hope Pass was like.

way waves remained to rock us through the night and at dawn a strong wind started up as we gathered on the roof. I can't say what the look on my face was because all the mirrors were down below, but the looks on the others were as kings, Teacher Rachel especially. Questions from clear eyes; maybe clearer channels for questions more open than we'd asked before.

'You're all looking at me.'

'You look ... there, Teacher Rachel,' I told her, 'or here. Here like never before. How do you feel?'

She reached out and held Mr. Ives' hand and said, 'I am still Teacher Rose, yet I do feel good and different.'

Our talk turned to the train. The water was spread out on the plain for as far as the eye could see, how deep way out there—I didn't know.

'Mr. Ives, can the train make it in here?'

'Um ...' He stood at the eave and studied from memory where the tracks ran up to the platform and beyond. 'Tracks are usually elevated above the ground and if you listen now, we have no more quakes, at least so far. I think it's a pretty good chance the engine and cars can make it in here and out again.'

'What are we going to send on the train?' I asked.
'Isabel?'
'What will we send in manifest?'
'Everyone had box hopes and were getting things together before the … the flood,' said Teacher Rachel.
'Well, I don't have anything. No baking done. Look out there at the arc booths, Teacher Rachel, what could be ready?'
'Some things, surely.'
'We better ask around.'
'Where will we put the goods that are brought in?' asked Mud Daisy Steve.

He and I descended into the water. When I reached the porch, I saw that water was still running out the door. The faucets were still open.

We stood in the Blass' yard and talked to Mr. Blass, who was leaning over the edge of his roof.

'What do you have for the train?'

He said that the boys had four boxes of tiles elevated down in the arc house and that was all. The two lads always made and cut tiles, carving the shapes of animals in them. Then they'd fill the animal reliefs with small turquoise stones they found on the plain. The animals stood bright in their tiles and the Blass boys, or I at least, thought that they'd be making those at Hope Pass and sending them out for years and years to come.

'How's your food?'
'We'll make it. Yours?'
"We'll make to too, Mr. Blass.'

We moved from arc house to arc house and it was the same—shared food, enough food, not much to export.

Once we were back on the boarding house, panic began to visit me for the first time. How on earth, I thought, were we to get full vats of water up on the roofs? And the food the train brought was fruit, not things to staple us.

I asked everyone to gather again so we could discuss this.

'It can't run forever,' said Mud Daisy Steve.

'How long, do you think?'

'I don't know. Mr. Ives?'

'There's no way of knowing. I told you it's a phenomenon.'

Indian Jon bent down to study the closer wells. 'They are still running.'

'My ... my ...' I said. 'How much of the world's water has come here?'

'Plenty,' said Mr. Ives.

'If the train comes, I must go on,' said Rose.

Those words made our soberness complete. Only a month, but that girl had been with us through some kind of month. Came riding in with an easel and pitch-pretty hair and another thing. It hurt me to think that we'd go back to before and that our ... this, Rose, didn't belong with us.

'We weren't very good hosts as it turned out, were we?' I asked, half serious, half pitying myself.

'Yes, you were. I feel I'm a Hope Passer, too, somehow.'

'You do?'

'Yes, Isabel, I do.'

'Indian Jon is going back to the mountains, of course,' I said.

'Uh huh. But I'll stay and help everyone clean up.'

'It's going to be bad down there,' said Teacher Rachel.

'I've been going back and forth on this—I'll be going on the train,' came from Mr. Ives.

'Ohhhhh ...'

'Isabel,' he said, 'you have been a gem to me. A solid gem. But I feel I must go.'

'Where?' asked Mud Daisy Steve.

'Van Horn, I suppose. For a while, anyway. That's where my deposits are. Then ... oh, then, get a feel for things.'

'What if they're flooded too?' I asked.

'Then farther, right away. And one day maybe come back. I think your house is more than we all can bear, Isabel.'

'I think so too, dearie Isabel. It's got to be a mess that would take years to—'

'You too, Teacher Rachel?'

'Isabel, maybe we all should go to Van Horn for a while. People can't work now ... my students can't learn now.'

'Steve?'

'I don't know what to do. I've been out there before and it didn't...'

'So, we're at this place.'

'Isabel, we've arrived here ... no one asked for it.'

'Outright, anyway,' said Mr. Ives. 'Hope Pass is much a home as any I've known. You caring for our needs. It's just too changed down there. Too much for people to do right now. We can't figure it'll be the same, you can't rest on something that itself doesn't rest.'

'Oh, Mr. Ives ...' And I was overcome.

'We can stay at Van Horn, at a hotel for a while. A month, say. Then we could get on the train for its next loop and come back and have a look.'

'If we come back to stay, we'd have to go on as before,' said Teacher Rachel, 'and no more cirl—'

I noticed Mud Daisy Steve lowering his head and shaking it back and forth.

'Do you think the others are thinking like this?'

Mr. Ives scratched his beard, looked at each of us in his turn, and said, 'I'll say it—circles and flood or a return to what it was before. Some choice.'

It was suggested that Teacher Rachel and I go down the ladder and find out exactly what the town was going to do, if they knew. We stood at the bases of arc houses, hollering up to the rooftops. When we returned to the roof of the boarding house, we made the consensus complete—we too decided to go.

While the others slept, I spent the night under a bright, round moon that arced right over the top of our roof. I could see the water out there on the plain and I could remember our sandstone beneath it and the song that used to play day and night. Again I thought about mama and papa. I felt little blame about leaving or about the town being scarred up so, nor did I understand my burden, my time, this flood that mama's and papa's memories didn't deserve. I'd long felt that with the paucity of children produced here the town would end up nearly uninhabited one day, but not a day this soon. But we'd kept on, always looking to the east, always hoping, hoping that that old train would bring us, us. Maybe it did, after all—this slight woman with the long locks who became one of our flower grower's own flowers.

And he, not so very different from the rest of us, lived by himself. But he set out to find out why and to send complete 'She loves me's' out to others so they might live that way. Tiles, human hair, pies, mystery bottles, yes, we sent out a number of things by those rails and we sent out hope for others, those flowers, I now saw. He asked Rose to show him if it worked, if his work was true, if the flowers only talked or if they meant it in the human world. I found out myself that they meant it. I'm one of the flowers now too. So is Teacher Rachel. Mrs. Blass. Others here, as well.

Hope flowers? Flowers of hope? If we return we can't be flowers anymore, we women. Our home or blooming in the pose of yes. Sad to choose.

Before the light came I planned for the journey ahead, first down to the boarding house and select what I'll take with me. Then, if I must get on that train, I'll go. I'll go to Van Horn and stay with my dears in another's hotel until the water recedes and my flowing is gone. And then I could come back here and fix up the house papa loved.

The first person to stir was Teacher Rachel. She was generous in her praise of me and my caring for her and being her friend for all the years. I demurred and stared at her. We used to sit out on the porch like we did and just be to each other. She talked about her students, literature, her family, or storytellers. I could only contribute my boarding house chores and what I'd gotten from Mr. Ives' newspapers and magazines. Then, later into the nights or on Saturdays, we'd look out onto the work booths or off to the old brick depot. I wonder now why we never could see through the depot to the platform where her singers would gather each month to sing in anticipation of hope, a box-full that never came.

Now we'd be out on that platform tomorrow and we'll be going to where the boxes came from. Outside this town, outside box hopes, I reckon.

ur flower grower was the first off the roof, stating that he had seeds to collect and his goodbyes to say. Indian Jon then descended the ladder to check on Bow and Arrow and he agreed to walk the town and make sure everyone knew that we were leaving on the train, if it came.

When I got inside the boarding house, I saw that Indian Jon had led his sopped horse into the dining room. I found a couple of damp-only towels in the pantry and dried as much of the animal as possible. He was fed the last of the oatmeal from the kitchen and his sodden eyes seemed to understand my soothing words.

The faucets still ran steady and the water was close to waste deep. In my room the wall hangings and the top dresser drawer had been spared a dunking. I took my portrait from the wall and the shawl photograph from the drawer and held them high above my head. Into the hall of life I sloshed, meeting Teacher Rachel and Mr. Ives, who went into their rooms to retrieve. I asked Indian Jon if he would enter Engineer Mert's room and take his name plaque off the wall. Rose passed me saying she'd get her easel and bags and soon start for the depot.

When we were all ready, each of us with an armload or

more and Indian Jon leading his horse, we formed some sort of soppy low and teary high parade that led through the town arc, scattered with toppled, mostly sunken arc booths, and on we went to the depot. We were met by others, Constable Betsy and Mr. O'Connell leading that parade.

There were many exposures on the platform, the beating sun and the water, knee deep out there, standing primary as the outer ones. Inner, for me, was the awareness that if we could come back, it would be as before, to live as before, before people turned to flowers and the houses to boats. All the years here, I'd thought I was no longer young, but that had been proven untrue only recently. If such a life's illusion could exist, I thought as I stood on the platform that day among the others, how many other ways had I been living that were also untrue? All the mirrors I'd hung in the boarding house, all the times I'd looked into those silvered clear mirrors—if the reflection from clear was false, the air between the reflection and I could not be too at fault. All the boxes I collected, a large family of them, sorted and stacked like in a cardboard morgue. All the boxes' contents over the years, pretty dolls and trinkets and the final poster of joy and loving couples. For what?

We expected to hear the whistle, but for several hours on the platform, it didn't sound. We'd look to the south or stand facing it hoping to see the high point of the engine emerge out of the sand on the horizon, moving on invisible tracks. And then it happened, we could see it moving slowly towards us. Still no whistle. We crowded near the edge of the platform as the three cars came nearer.

"Be patient,' someone said, 'He'll be passing and have to back up anyway.'

Then the train slowed to a crawl and we could see Engineer Mert clearly through his window. And the dear man brought the cars to a halt, flush with the platform boards.

I caught myself looking at others' faces, trying to see if

there was glee at this train stop. Engineer Mert jumped down into the water, swiveling his head all around at us, at the town, then at the old brick depot, and again he repeated this viewing sequence.

I approached him and handed him his and his father's plaque. His turreting head stopped its movement and he stared down at the words while moving his fingers softly across the embedded turquoise stones.

'I've never touched it before,' he said.

He looked a 'thank you' back to me and turned and opened the passenger car doors and said that it was as dry in there as we looked to be wet. People helped the children up the steps first and water ran down their clothing to their shoes and on down to the platform. I stood back a bit and watched Hope Passers, one by one, and silently, climb up into the car with armloads of all they had left.

When Constable Betsy was about to board, I gave her a hug and said that we'd all do well in Van Horn. She held me close for a moment and then said that she and Mr. O'Connell would be moving on into central Texas to find Ellie, who was working a big carnival there.

When it came time for Teacher Rachel to board, she stopped next to me.

'Isabel, Mr. Ives and I are going somewhere. He said he has enough funds in the bank and that it's enough for me too. He says we should get it and go somewhere fresh for a while. That Van Horn is too memory-close for now. I can care for him and help him with his cussing,' she grinned.

'Yes, you can, dearie.'

Mr. Ives nodded his head at me and said he could help me out if I needed it. And he said 'Thank you for the true home.' And then he boarded.

I turned to Rose, who kissed me on the cheek. She said that Mud Daisy Steve and she were going together, wherever they were going. She said Hope Pass made her feel all the way, no more halfway Rose.

I stood alone on the platform and looked past the depot and the town arc and could see my boarding house in the distance. As I turned back toward the train, my eyes landed on Indian Jon who sat astride Bow and Arrow just off the platform. He turned to his side and untied straps on the horse's back and then tossed two packs into the water while he looked at me. He ran his hand across the horse where the packs had been.

I turned once more and looked at the town, at the boarding house, at mama and papa standing on the porch waving at me. I took a step toward the horse and stopped. Were they waving for me to come back or waving goodbye? I looked at Indian Jon again and waded toward him.

I handed him my portrait and the satchel of dresser drawer things and he pulled me up onto the horse's back.

I saw that noses were pressed to the glass inside the passenger car, but through the steam that blurred the windows, I couldn't tell how many were looking at me on the horse and how many were looking beyond to their town.

Engineer Mert hollered from his engine that he'd be back next month, that if his train could swim like this, heck, he'd be back every month forever. He then stoked the engine and it started to chug past the platform and away from two people on a horse heading due north.

My arms held onto Indian Jon as his horse waded out of Hope Pass and into more of the ocean on the plain. We watched as the train grew smaller and smaller and then all that remained was water. I tried not to turn around but once I pulled at Indian Jon's shirt so he would stop.

The town looked bright and half sunken. The structures rising out of the water looked like atolls I had seen pictures of in Mr. Ives' magazines. At a distance, I could see how the buildings had been turned around some. I thought about the graves, mama's and papa's and the others, and about all the hopes our dead had passed down to us, we who are leaving now.

The water grew shallower as we neared the peaks and when I looked to my right, I could see train tracks lying on top of sand before they disappeared from sight.

I could always send word, I thought, once I return and get the boarding house up and running again. Teacher Rachel will write —yes, she'll come back. And Mr. Ives with her. Mud Daisy Steve, he'll surely write to me and I can tell him it 's all right to return. And Rose, too! Yes, Rose can come back. I can get everyone back. But wait, what if they continue with the new practice? Maybe they'd be scared of another flood. That choice may always be necessary.

When we arrived at the foothills where the ground was merely moist, Indian Jon stopped, reached back, and helped me down from the horse. He dismounted, tended to Bow and Arrow and then withdrew his pipe from inside his shirt. We sat cross-legged, smoking while looking out onto the plain and a thin mist rising off the water. Indian Jon sang an Awoik song and then we sat in silence still looking out, maybe in, for the remainder of the afternoon.

When we arrived at his home, he brought out salted meat and some berries. He told me that his tepee was my tepee, that I could stay in the mountains as long as I liked and that he'd take me back to Hope Pass or even up to Van Horn whenever I wanted to leave.

I learned many things from him during the first weeks up here. He showed me a lookout from which I could see the outline of Hope Pass and I took to spending a portion of each afternoon doing just that. The water stayed for months; a couple short of a year I believe.

My companion is quiet and even more slow moving than Hope Passers had been. He seemed to be a bush when near a bush, a stream when near one of those. He began to feel to me like part of the mountains, part of every thing up here. Once, after smoking with him, I realized that some, him at least, at some stage in the development of their fickle human hearts, get a notion, turn and try to secede from the viscous growing mass, but are stymied during the revolt leaving them still attached to the great invisible by the narrowest of trachea. I came to feel close to the Indian. I can't call him my Indian but what he did show, what he did say and do was enough because it was real.

Because I couldn't bring myself to do it, he went down to Hope Pass once the water was gone and brought back the report that several feet of mud lay on the ground and in the boarding house. He retrieved some of my things that first time and said he'd found Mama's rocking chair washed up against the train depot. He put it in my room.

Twice I'd seen the train as it left Hope Pass and headed north, and after some months had passed, I asked Indian Jon if he'd go down and meet Engineer Mert and find out if there were letters from anyone.

When he returned he told me that Engineer Mert sent his greetings but that there were no letters. They made arrangements by which anything we sent out or were to receive would be placed under the fourth north board of the train platform. Under that board is where he placed the deed to the boarding house that I'd long before had drawn up. It was to go to a niece who last I'd heard lived in Colorado. I guess I should apologize for the condition of the boarding house but it was all unforeseen of course.

My companion says he'll check the fourth board again next month and I'll have him take this journal and my shawl photograph down and put them in the top drawer of my dresser. That way, if any relatives ever take the muddy old place, at least they'll know how it got to be such a mess and why people left the town.

So far, I received no word from my boarders or from Rose or anyone. Indian Jon says no one has returned to Hope Pass and I think I know why.

For me, I've decided to live here in these two mountains in a life of circling and making my own inner hope. My portrait hangs on a pole inside our tepee and her eyes remain clear.

Isabel Ritter
1951

So I found that the people who had lived here went to the end. They'd put their lives' hopes in boxes from a train, Aunt Isabel's hopey, dreamy way. Then left. From all appearances, no one returned here, no town at all anymore.

I closed the leather journal for the last time and sat for a long time in the old rocker that barely held on to that name. As I looked around the room at wall hangings, sandblasted to hell and back and at the dresser, she came more into view even if she'd taken her clear-eyed portrait. She'd left behind the photo of herself in the shawl and the shawl itself, and I'll take them home with me.

The other people she spoke of are less clear to me though some of their words stay with me. *Rested on. Can't rest on something that doesn't its self rest.* Mr. Ives' words. These people had rested on box hopes for so long until they had to move on. Cardboard boxes full of hope.

I tucked the journal under my arm and took a last walk around the town that was. When I got to the north edge of town, through the song that played off the sands, I looked at the two mountains off in the distance. They looked exactly alike, twin risings grown round with nipple-shaped peaks looking up to the sky. Before I left, I entered the tattered arc house that belonged to Mud Daisy Steve. I found packets of dried seeds so I put a couple of them in my pocket. I'd never heard of them but their inventor might have given them up once he left here. He had another kind of flower to tend to, the journal says.

I returned to my home and its jagged hum. I tried to let go of Hope Pass and go back to my life of trying, but what had happened there haunted me. I'd had a glimpse of a perfect thing and of the opening that leads to it. I desperately wanted to find out if Aunt Isabel spoke the truth.

She, my wife, listened to the story of Hope Pass with a 10-gallon hat full of skepticism. But she said she'd try it. It didn't work the first couple of times and my doubts grew. And then, it happened—she posed in full circle. No flood ensued, to be sure, but she drained and gushed and left for a spell. When she came back to herself, her thirst was enormous and we were both a little different afterward. And now that we know how, we're a lot wetter and know that this pose has something that only trying cannot feel.

I planted the seeds I'd brought back and they grew into "She loves me … She loves me," each and every one. They are perfectly round and glow in the moonlight.

The journal and the shawl, which I hung over a window, remained on my mind and I decided to again take the route I'd taken months before.

We packed and then drove southeast and into Texas. This time I steered to the base of the twin peaks. We hiked for several hours and finally came to a camp comprised of a large tepee, meat-drying racks, a small cone-shaped structure, hides stretched out on poles and two horses nearby.

There was a slow, steady beat overhead and when I looked for it, straight up through the top of the clearing where this camp stood, there were the peaks, perfectly matched and rising into the clouds.

A low voice came from inside the tepee and we neared it.

"Hello?" I said.

Out of the tepee walked a bent old Indian looking up at Sarah and me through his eyebrows.

"No one comes up here."

I reached for Sarah's hand to comfort her, us.

"Are you Indian Jon?" I asked.

He continued his expressionless look.

"Are you Indian Jon, the Awoik?"

At this, his face moved a little and he took a step back. He leaned his back against the tepee and raised his neck as far up as it would go, looking at the sky or the peaks up there.

"I am Indian Jon, the last Awoik. The first of the Awoiks, and the last."

"Just as she'd written!" I cried inside. Right there, I stood facing the former visitor to Hope Pass. I wanted to blurt out many questions but I kept them down.

"Indian Jon, last of the Awoiks, we came to find out about my Aunt Isabel Ritter."

He looked into my eyes. The deep wrinkles that mapped his face all seemed to home in on me, those words I'd spoken. He was reading me closely.

"My Aunt Isabel who used to have the boarding house down there in Hope Pass."

"Yea, she did."

"You knew her well?"

"Still do"

"She's—"

"I'm in mourning now."

"Ohhh ..."

"Come."

He turned to his right and slowly led us past the cone structure and onto a thin, well-worn path. On either side were pine trees that gave the path the scent of an aisle. Before long, it opened onto a circular plot of ground with stones laid out all around, serving as a border. At the center of this spot, there was a group of large stones placed in a circular mount. Indian Jon pointed to this and shook his head up and down. I saw tears run down his cheeks and I somehow knew why.

He turned to us, nodded his head distinctly in the direction from which we'd walked, and Sarah and I followed him back to his camp.

When there, he pulled back the flap to the tepee and waved his arm for us to enter. There was a fire burning and meat cooking on it. Then, I saw a large framed picture hanging on one of the tepee poles. I got close and saw a woman sitting in a rocking chair. I squinted to recognize. Then they grabbed me. Those eyes. They looked out at me like crystals gleaming out of a pool of water. I blinked and almost expected them to do the same. I turned and looked at Sarah to see if her eyes were clear, clearer than before. They were and I hadn't noticed since she'd begun to pose her pudenda in the perfect way.

Indian Jon sat down near the fire and motioned for us to sit across from him. He offered food and then lit his pipe while we nibbled on a rabbit. Then we all smoked and he sang a song that I couldn't understand the words to but it sounded sad.

"Yea, Isabel had the boarding house down there. I used to go there one time every year. One year a stranger came, sent by the Great Mother. She showed us where we were. Who we were also. The stranger showed us how to wake up the Mother and the Mother rejoiced. She sent water. It went into their houses. They grew scared. They left. Isabel came here to my home. Here we lived on another part of the Mother."

"What was she like?"

"Is like."

"Is?"

"She left our tepee one month ago. You saw her under the stones but she still lives here."

"A month? Only a month?"

"Yea."

"I could have ... What was she like?"

"She was all the time busy down there. Here she found slow. She learned the ways of the Awoik. She was a good woman. That's what she taught me."

"Indian Jon, I received a deed to the boarding house and went to Hope Pass a couple of months ago."

"I know those things."

"You do?"

"I mailed the deed long ago. I felt someone down there recently. Now I know it was you."

"I read the journal she wrote."

"I made that for her."

"It told about her life in Hope Pass, others' lives, told about you. The flood. The train. The board. The fourth board."

"I used to go down there and check under the board for her. No mail ever came for her."

"Nothing?"

"No. She used to Awoik pray for mail from Mud Daisy Steve, Teacher Rachel, Mr. Ives, Rose the Stranger. She never gave up praying that they'd get mail to her or that they'd come back."

"All those years?"

"Yea."

"Does the train still stop there?"

"Yea. We've seen it plenty. There is a new driver now."

"Does he—"

"I don't know if it's been passed to him. I don't go down now. Ever. I'm old. I'm an old man now. I'm a wise old elder Indian man now."

"Yes. Yes you are."

"There are none to follow me. There are no other Awoiks except Isabel and me."

Sarah and I gathered firewood and carried a week's supply of it into the tepee. After we'd said our goodbyes and had started back down the mountains, I stopped. We turned around and reentered the camp. Indian Jon was still standing outside his tepee.

"Indian Jon, I want to know if you'll come and live with us in our place. There are mountains there—high ones—and you'll be welcome."

He stepped toward me until our faces were nearly touching. "You are like your Aunt. But this is my home. Her home. We're close to the Mother. I must live the Awoik way. When I'm gone, the Awoik is gone."

The look in his eye was inscrutable, and though I was tempted to think he wanted us to stay, I can't say for sure.

The mud daisies are thriving and there has been no variation in their message. Sarah and I often make circles and water and we just as often talk about going to Hope Pass and restoring the boarding house. There is train service there and plenty of water. And I want to look under that fourth board to the North. But then we'd take the chance of causing another flood, for the pose they'd learned at Hope Pass and which Sarah and I now practice is not something we can stop doing. Then we talk about going up to those two mountains and learning Awoik ways before it is too late, too late again.

-The End-